THE COURAGEOUS

REBELS

BOOK TWO OF THREE

THE COURAGEOUS

Dafydd ab Hugh

POCKET BOOKS
New York London Toronto Sydney Tokyo Singapore

An *Original* Publication of POCKET BOOKS

POCKET BOOKS, a division of Simon & Schuster Inc.
1230 Avenue of the Americas, New York, NY 10020

This book is published by Pocket Books, a division of Simon & Schuster Inc., under exclusive license from Paramount Pictures.

ISBN: 0-671-01141-3

First Pocket Books printing February 1999

10 9 8 7 6 5 4 3 2 1

Printed in the U.S.A.

Historian's Note

The present-day sections of the Rebels trilogy take place during the fourth season of *Star Trek: Deep Space Nine*.

THE COURAGEOUS

CHAPTER 1

THIRTY YEARS AGO

THE BULLETIN-TEA in Legate Migar's headquarters droned on and on, stretching into its fourth tedious hour. Sister Winn and the other Bajoran servants—Shimpur Anan, who served Gul Feesat; Lisea Nerys and Alahata-something, who were brought down to the planet by Gul Dukat; and the six servants of Legate Migar who cooked and served the food (one was a true collaborator, Winn was certain)—were at last allowed to eat their own lunch in the kitchen . . . after they had waited upon the high-ranking Cardassians, served, fetched, and cleared away.

Alone with themselves now, the Bajorans let their bitterness erupt; *like a baby spitting up,* thought Sister Winn, surprising herself with her own cynicism. Alahata spoke of his anger at servitude. He was nearly as young as Gul Ragat, but he had grown up in a village not far from Winn's, Riesentaka on the Heavenly Blue River. Winn tried to calm him with homilies from the Prophets, but the boy would not be placated. *He'll learn,* she thought in sadness, noting the interest of two of Legate Migar's valets, one of whom was probably the snitch.

The others spoke of domestic issues. Nerys was worried about the rains, which had come too soon for her father's farm. But even in the simplest conversation, Sister Winn could practically cut the tension with a knife—if Bajorans in service to a gul had been allowed knives. They each knew who and what they were, and how precarious was the thread by which their world dangled.

The Bajorans fell silent as Winn blessed the food, and they ate; the food was too rich for the priestess, not the simple, country fare she had grown up with, but the elaborate, spicy meats the Cardassians preferred among Bajoran foods—*food from the Northern Islands,* Winn said to herself. Her mother had come from there, but her father had forbidden spice in the family meals, as he had a weak stomach.

The kitchen was gigantic but cozy. Legate Migar had not built his own house, but taken over the house of the original governor of the subcontinent, Riasha Lyas. Riasha had disappeared thirteen years ago and was rumored to have been sent up to *Terok Nor;* but no one who returned from the station orbiting Bajor had ever reported seeing him. A stained-glass window facing northwest allowed in much natural light in the afternoon, but Winn could not see outside. A smaller, plain window set above the stained glass afforded an abbreviated view . . . assuming the priestess were to stand on a chair. The men used the plain window to look out for arriving VIPs.

Red and blue shadows crossed the kitchen table as Winn pushed her food from one side of the plate to the other, hoping to fool the cook into thinking she had enjoyed the meal. She answered automatically whenever one of the other Bajorans would ask her religious advice, or beg for a prayer or benediction for the weather, the crops, a sick cousin, the soul of Bajor. But she smiled and turned her face full on whoever was speaking, seeming to give undivided attention; inside, Sister Winn was thinking dark thoughts and wondering how she could pull off her mission without ending up the Headless Sister of Shakarri.

At last, the table was cleared by the probable collaborator, whose name she learned at last: Revosa Anan. She filed away the information for future use. Sister Winn rose, gave a final blessing and thanks to the Prophets, and bowed her way out of the kitchen, saying she had to return and see if her master needed anything.

She stepped lightly toward the conference room

but paused in the courtyard; no one appeared to be watching; the house felt heavy, sleepy after the midday meal. Bowing her head and walking with a firm step, Sister Winn turned to the right and cut across the short angle of the courtyard toward a small, forbidden door she had observed from its other side when she first arrived at Legate Migar's palace. The door opened to her firm touch; she entered, smiling and readying an obsequious apology if she ran into an overly dutiful Cardassian guard. Not that an apology would matter. If the door turned out to lead where she prayed it did, and she were caught inside, then the next stop would surely be *Terok Nor* . . . and Gul Dukat's tender ministry.

Sister Winn entered the small antechamber that led to the formal reception room, and in the other direction, to the entrance hall. The walls were done in bloodwood paneling, very dark, and the only light came from two "electric candle" light fixtures at opposite sides of the outer wall. Between the fixtures was another door, this one soundproofed and sealed with a push-button combination lock popular among the erstwhile Bajoran military missions . . . like the house of Governor Riasha.

Swallowing hard, the priestess approached the lock. Her steps faltered. If she were caught in the next few seconds, no amount of bowing and scraping could save her from interrogation, followed by execution—and disgrace and exile for Gul Ragat;

but quite frankly, Sister Winn could not have cared less what happened to her Cardassian "master." His own conscience was in the hands of the Prophets; either he would see and save himself, or he would remain in ignorance and be forever barred from their embrace.

The strangest thing about Cardassians, Winn pondered, *is how thoroughly they believe their rules of conquered and conquerer!* They had won the battle; they had won the war. Simple honor among soldiers required that the Bajorans accept their status and work to achieve full recognition as eventual citizens of the Cardassian Empire.

It certainly never occurred to Legate Migar to run around replacing all the locks in his house. It never penetrated his bony Cardassian skull that although poor Governor Riasha was probably in the arms of the Prophets a decade since, and the officers of the Bajoran Army were all executed or imprisoned in penal colonies or mines around the planet and even on *Terok Nor,* that many of the governor's former *civilian engineers* had also worked in the palace . . . and some had frequent occasion to work in the communications room. And the legate, who had never been any kind of an engineer, civilian or military, was evidently unaware of the disdain with which such people treat security precautions.

In particular, Legate Migar had never heard of a lock having a "back door," used by the engineers if the military men changed the lock and neglected to tell the civilian contractors. He had ordered the combination altered, of course; but he never realized that there was *more than one combination.*

Licking her dry lips, Sister Winn took a deep breath, stepped up to the lock, and punched in the back-door code she had received from her cell leader. The lock clicked twice, and the red lights on the side turned green. Sister Winn pressed firmly on the door, and it pushed noiselessly open, exposing a dark room whose walls were lined with communications equipment. In front of the six chairs were lists of common frequencies, map displays, and miracle of the Prophets, a current *codebook!*

Please protect me, she begged; then she stepped into the room, pushing the door nearly shut, and felt in the heel of her knee boot for the tiny, digital holocam she had carried for four months, waiting for just such an opportunity. The bright displays beckoned, but Sister Winn knew her first goal; she activated the codebook and began to click through it, snapping pictures of every screen.

When Sister Winn finally finished holocamming the book, a wave of relief flooded her brain. She wasn't "off the mountain," as her villagers used to say; she still had to exit without losing the holocam and get the images to her cell—or some cell, at least. But at least, even if she got nothing else, her mission was successful.

But in a lapse of security that would be incredible to anyone who hadn't lived with the Cardassians for years and didn't know the depth of their disdain for the "lesser races," the communications room remained unattended for another ten minutes. During that time, Winn took holopictures of every screen and all the frequency settings; she even dared project different maps on the coder's viewer and holocammed them as well; though her mouth was so dry, she was having trouble breathing. If there were a history file, somebody was going to be awfully suspicious . . . and if there were security viewers, she could be under fatal observation as she brought up map after map, caught and convicted by her own hand.

Then Winn heard what she had expected to hear minutes earlier: the bootsteps of the Cardassian guard returning on his rounds. With a lot less coolness than she would have liked, she rested her boot on the console and rotated the heel outward with trembling fingers. She replaced the holocam and swung the heel shut, hearing it lock into place. She exited the room just as the guard turned the corner, but she didn't dare pull the door shut . . . the guard would hear the click of the lock and be alerted.

He paused when he saw her standing with her back to the communications room door, staring with a vacant expression as if she were in a trance. "Bajoran slave! What are *you* doing here?" he demanded.

Winn turned toward the guard, blinking as if she

had never seen a Cardassian before in her life and wasn't quite sure whether it was alive or not. "Sir?" she asked, striving for an intelligence level somewhere above imbecile but well below normal.

The Cardassian was only too happy to oblige, seeing her as a conquered "animal." He spoke very slowly, enunciating every word in Bajoran (but with a barbarous accent). "Why—are—you—here?"

Winn brightened. "Oh! Can you help me? My master needs the activity reports on Resistance action for the last month. He's very important."

"Activity reports? I don't know anything about that! I have received no word. Who is your master?" He paused, and Winn stared at him uncomprehendingly. *"Who—is—your—MASTER?"* shouted the impatient guard, raising his clenched fist.

The priestess cringed away from the man, burying her face in her hands and falling heavily to her knees. "Please don't hurt me! My master is Gul Ragat, subgovernor of Shakarri and Belshakarri! He is here to meet with their lordships Legate Migar and Gul Dukat for the bulletin-tea."

The guard, wearing the uniform of a sergeant major and carrying only a hand disruptor at his belt, paused to ponder the new information. He was evidently aware of the bulletin-teas, but didn't seem to know for sure which guls were on the invitation list. "Well," he snarled, "where are you supposed to find this report? You're not allowed to be in this part of the building!"

"Please, sir! My master told me to report to the duty officer of the communications room."

The sergeant's gaze strayed immediately to the door, still open a crack. His eyes widened. "What—!" Rushing to the door, he threw it open, seeing only the dark room with a few illuminated controls and the main viewer showing the Cardassian insignia, the neutral "background" image when nothing else was displayed.

A moment later, he returned to the hall, staring down at Sister Winn with a new light of crafty intelligence. "Did you enter this room, Bajoran?"

"I wanted to," she blurted out, "but I was too afraid! I don't know what the report looks like, and—and I was afraid to go poking around where I wasn't—I didn't know what to do, so I just waited until . . ." Winn began to sniffle, making herself cry real tears and sneeze; it was a talent she had learned as a child, always good for eliciting sympathy from sympathetic adults. It didn't work quite as well against Cardassian conquerers; but still, it was the only weapon she had. Her knees hurt, which helped the deception.

"Look, stop that sniveling! Did—you—enter—this—*room?* Just answer the question!"

Winn shook her head vigorously. "No, sir, but I . . ."

"Yes?"

"I didn't, but I . . ."

"You WHAT?" The sergeant major was rapidly losing what tiny bit of patience he had.

"I—I—*I touched the door!* Oh, Prophets preserve me, I pushed it, and it swung a little, and I—I *looked inside for a minute!"*

The guard sighed and seemed to slump a little. He looked away, starting to be embarassed by the sight of a but still somewhat pretty, young woman sobbing hysterically on the floor. The priestess peeked through her fingers and saw the man chewing his lip and staring at the door; *probably wondering whether he's going to get in trouble over the open door,* she understood.

"Stupid civilian com-techies," he muttered in Cardassian. Then he looked back over his own shoulder, reached out, and pulled the door shut tightly. "Look, you couldn't get the report thing you wanted because there wasn't anyone in the room. You got that? *Do—you—underSTAND?"* The sergeant major nodded his head affirmatively.

"There wasn't . . . I couldn't get the report?" Winn put on a look of bewilderment.

"There—wasn't—anyone—here! Oh, for goodness sake, it's so——easy!" He used an obscenity Winn had heard before, but only from lower-class Cardassian soldiers.

"Oh! I couldn't get the report because . . . because . . ." Winn paused, tapping her forehead as if thinking through the scheme. ". . . there was nobody in the room!"

"Yes!" he exclaimed, pushing her back against the wall. "Open your foolish Bajoran ears next time! And"—he leaned close to snarl directly in the priestess's face—"don't you *ever* push open a door like that again! *Never!* You understand me?" For emphasis, he put his metal-shod boot on Sister Winn's back; she made no move to push it away, merely drawing back in terror, and the sergeant major didn't put his weight on it, either.

"Yes, sir! I understand, sir! Thank you, sir!"

He let her up but made no move to help; Winn rose shakily to her feet, bowed and cringed in the most servile manner she could manage, and backed away—still bowing and thanking him for correcting her. As soon as she rounded the same corner whence the guard had come, she turned and bustled as fast as she could manage to the "allowed" section of Legate Migar's house. She didn't meet any more Cardassian guards along the way; this deep inside the pale, the gul had no fear of Resistance action, and he seemed to take an austere pride in living virtually alone with his family and only a skeleton force of soldiers. She had already returned to the conference room, where her master was desperately trying not to nod off during an interminable supply report by Gul Feesat before the reality struck her full, starting her trembling all over again: *I did it!* she screamed inside her mind; *I actually did it and got away!*

But another voice answered back, the voice she usually used to correct her behavior when she violated the word or spirit of the Prophets: *You've not gotten away yet, child; or haven't you noticed whose house this still is?*

She couldn't help smiling, praying that the worst was over. But her inner nag warned that the worst had just begun. Sister Winn was now officially "hangable."

The young Gul Ragat was still brooding over his possible elevation, and annoyed that nobody mentioned anything at the bulletin-tea about it: Legate Migar and Gul Dukat simply spoke to him as they normally did, with no special winks or nods, nothing to indicate it was other than ordinary that Ragat be invited to such an unordinary meeting. He complained—or hinted at his irritation, actually—to Sister Winn in a long soliloquy in the garden that evening, while Winn did her best to appear sympathetic and hopeful.

Her own agenda was somewhat different. "My Lord," she said soothingly, "I'm sure you were right in your original thought, that you are being groomed for the higher grant of honors. Surely you see the hand of the Prophets in this?"

"The Prophets?" Gul Ragat blinked at Winn. "I don't quite follow. How do the Bajoran Prophets figure into my elevation?"

"They know what a compassionate man m'lord is; they must know that of all the Cardassians, Gul Ragat is most concerned about the physical *and spiritual* ills of the Bajoran people! Surely they have brought your qualities to the attention of Legate Migar for a reason."

Ragat paced agitatedly. "A reason? Because I

will be a more compassionate master than, say, Gul Dukat, with his iron fist and heart of stone?"

"Oh, you most certainly would be." She wondered whether he would catch the significance of the reference to the spiritual ills; Winn had heard that somewhere in the Cardassian Empire, scattered and powerless but there, was a group of Cardassians who argued bitterly against the occupation of Bajor, and indeed all the other planets forcibly "civilized" into the empire. She knew Gul Ragat was not a member of that outlawed group—he certainly wouldn't be given even a subgovernorship if there were the slightest hint in his background check!—but if Winn had heard of them, then Ragat had heard of them . . . and she would not give up hope that the Prophets would in time lead those Cardassians with even the slightest hint of decency to the moral position.

"Yes," he mused, "I suppose I could do much to alleviate the needless suffering of your people, were I to be granted a higher position in the administration of Bajor."

"My Lord," said Sister Winn, bowing her head and looking intently at her feet, "may I speak frankly?"

"Of course, of course! I allow all my servants the freedom to say what is truly on their minds, in private."

"My Lord, if your people continue along this path they have chosen, there will certainly be bloody resistance against Cardassian rule. My Bajorans are a proud people, and we do not take well to the leash."

"Winn, you are a priestess! A spiritual leader! How can you threaten such a terrible thing?"

You young fool! "My Lord, I do not threaten; I predict. I know my own. And I know that a few hundred thousand Cardassian troops will not hold against an entire planetful of bitter, determined freedom fighters. I shudder at the images my mind conjures, fantastic scenarios of mass destruction. But I cannot turn my face from the inevitable."

Gul Ragat turned his back to Sister Winn. "I cannot listen to a prediction of such betrayal! Sister, I'm surprised at you, giving credence to the juvenile boasting of that Resistance rabble. You know what would happen: those who revolted would be wiped out, as well as their family and probably their friends, even if innocent."

The garden was dark and cool, but Winn saw it full of menace and unfriendly, grasping tree branches—though it was the same, friendly garden as in the days of Riasha Lyas. Evil had escaped from the Cardassian garrison inside the house and permeated the trimmed paths and hedgerows of the pastoral arboretum. "And it would be such a waste of resources," sighed the young subgovernor, almost to himself.

Winn was glad the garden was dark, so Gul Ragat could not see her rolling her eyes in disgust. She quickly and silently apologized to Those who *did* see, because They saw all. Then her young "master" made one more offhand remark that electrified the priestess: "Perhaps it would secure my advancement and serve the true interests of your people both," he mused, "if I were to bring in a few of these rabble-rousers myself . . . the ones who incite peaceful Bajorans to bloody revolution and cause us no end of trouble."

There was nothing, *nothing* that Sister Winn wanted more desperately than to get away from Legate Migar's palace and relocate somewhere she could pass along the priceless content of her holocam. But Bajoran servants—*slaves,* she corrected herself unemotionally—simply did not travel alone without travel documents issued by the Cardassian Planetary Authority . . . not even priestesses on a religious mission. There were only two ways for Winn to remove herself from Migar's estate without exciting attention: get her gul or another, higher-ranking gul to send her on an errand; or else, get Gul Ragat to travel with her.

The first was virtually impossible; anything important enough to go get was by and large too important for a Cardassian to leave to a Bajoran. The invaders had skimmers; they had shuttles; they had starships with beaming facilities. If Gul Ragat really wanted something physical, an artisan's vase or a barrel of sunberry wine, he would either transport it to him or transport himself to it; he would not send Sister Winn.

But if Ragat wanted to *personally capture* some antiCardassian Resistance leaders—especially without alerting other guls who might want to elbow into the credit—he was pretty much restricted to moving by skimmer, as he came . . . and moving his entire entourage in the direction of home. Anything less, or moving in any other direction, and the Planetary Authority would demand *his* travel documents! Since he didn't have enough skimmers for everyone, he and his household would ride, while everyone else, Cardassian honor guard and Bajoran domestics, would go as they had come, on foot, as befit their station as a subject race.

It's amazing how many opportunities a lengthy walk presents, thought the priestess craftily. But before she could plan an escape or rendezvous, she first had to start the wheels in motion: Winn had to persuade Gul Ragat to take the trip in the first place.

"My Lord, I . . ." Winn trailed off, then tried to look as though she had said nothing.

"Yes, Sister Winn?" Gul Ragat waited; Winn could feel the tension in his body, and she realized she had struck just the right tone: *I've got a terrible secret, but I don't know whether I can tell you!*

She fidgeted. She opened her mouth and sucked in a breath, then let it out without saying anything. "You can tell me anything when we're alone," soothed the gul, deliberately standing far enough away from her that she wouldn't feel crowded. Again, the priestess almost spoke and didn't.

Finally, she pretended to come to a resolution.

She sat slowly on the bench, despite the fact that her gul was standing . . . a terrible breach of protocol! "My Lord, I know of a rise that's planned for a few days from now—but I cannot tell, I cannot! Not even to secure your advancement."

Now, Gul Ragat couldn't contain himself. He spun to face her and asked breathlessly, "You do? You know? You have? You will?"

"I cannot violate the trust of my people, even if it means your grant of honors, Gul Ragat. I just can't!" *Come along, child . . . convince me!*

The gul stepped back, seeming to stop himself by brute force from grabbing Winn's shoulders and shaking her vigorously. "But, Winn—Sister Winn . . . you wouldn't be doing it for *me;* you'd be doing it to help your own people!"

"My own people? How do you mean?" She allowed a note of hope to creep into her voice.

"Your own people, whom you would save from the brutal retaliation sure to be inflicted upon them by the harsh and stern military leaders of the Empire! Imagine what will happen to the Bajorans living in that province or prefecture if you allow this insane rebellion to proceed!"

Sister Winn gasped. "I never thought of that."

"You must! You must think on it, and you will see that the only thing to do is to tell me now, quickly, so I can stop the troubles from ever starting by arresting the callous, uncaring leaders."

"Must I?"

Ragat shook his head sadly, sorrowing with her,

not at her. "There is no other honorable course for you to take. You are a leader, the voice of the Prophets. You must look after your—your flock; yes, that's the word. They look to you for guidance! Exercise your moral leadership to lead them to acceptance of the inevitable, and think of how much happier they will be."

Sister Winn suddenly jumped to her feet, pretending guilt at suddenly realizing she was sitting while her "master" stood. "Forgive me, My Lord!" she cried; Gul Ragat waved away the infraction, intent upon the information she might give him. Winn felt like a fisherman reeling in her catch.

The problem, Winn realized nervously, was that she actually *had* the information to give. In her position as spiritual leader for all the Bajorans who lived at Ragat's compound and many in the village of Vir-Hakar, in the county of Belshakarri, she always heard rumors of Resistance activity . . . often well-founded. She knew, for instance, that there was a planned meeting in precious Riis, a meeting that would probably lead to action against the spaceport ten kilometers away—a facility now used by the Cardassians to transport high-ranking members of the military and important visitors to and from the planet. A bombing was likely, and a full-scale assault was not out of the question.

It was the only such action that she knew of; if she wanted to give Ragat something he could substantiate—and it was clear he would check it out through his own intelligence network—there was nothing else for her to give. The attack could probably be postponed without much danger, *if* she got word to the Resistance in time! If not . . . then Sister Winn would have just committed a real, honest-to-Prophets act of collaboration which would surely result in the violent deaths of many Bajoran freedom fighters. It was a terrible choice!

But really, she thought anxiously, *I have no choice.* With the information digitized in her holocam, such blows could be struck as to completely eclipse the strike at the Riis Spaceport, called the Palm of Bajor. If she could get the holocam to her cell leader; as always, *IF!*

"My Lord," she whispered, "I have heard that there is to be a rising very near to here."

"Yes?"

"Between here and our own home, in fact."

"Yes?" Gul Ragat's excitement was palpable; Winn fought hard to keep her expression neutral, her eyes cast respectfully downward, and to sniffle a bit.

"It will be in—in Riis. That is what I heard."

"Riis? On the Shakiristi River?"

"That is what I heard, M'Lord."

Now Ragat sat suddenly, wearing a goofy grin and staring into space . . . *staring at his grant of honors,* thought the priestess bitterly. After a moment, he remembered himself and grew solemn. "You have done a noble and brave thing, Sister

Winn. You have saved many of your people from a terrible fate. The Prophets would be proud of you . . . I'm certain of it."

Oh Prophets, she prayed, *please grant me that same certainty!* But the Prophets, as was often the case, remained as mute as the stones on the issue.

Once more, Kai Winn woke in the night, the tendrils of the past wrapped around her. Now, at least, she knew there was some reason—that the Prophets were sending her a message, something that she must, must, be clever enough to grasp.

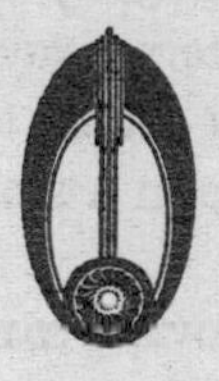

CHAPTER 2

"LISTEN UP, away team," said Captain Sisko, standing before his away team on a dark red bluff overlooking a shady, indigo valley; Worf came to attention, awaiting the new orders. A hundred meters below them, "Mayor-General" Asta-ha and her commandos—the Terrors of Tiffnaki, the name suggested by the hereditary mayor's daughter Tivva-ma—ran the rest of the Tiffnakis through a heavy set of drills, trying to beat into their posteconomic heads some sense of the danger they were in. Worf had designed the drills himself, and he was pleased at how quickly the Natives were learning how to fight as a unit.

"All right," asked the captain, "what's it going to be, then? We cannot reach the main planetary power stations and destroy them on foot; they're thousands of kilometers away. We need transporation, and the *Defiant* seems to have left orbit. So, do we try to overwhelm a small patrol by force or by stealth?"

Days earlier, the away team had finally left the natives of Sierra-Bravo to continue training themselves, for all the good that would do. Worf had few doubts what he would find upon his return: ragged, threadbare, unarmed, frightened, cowering, starving refugees crouching in the bushes like animals. But what could he do, stay forever with Asta-ha and her "Terrors" of Tiffnaki? The captain was right: it was time the Starfleet team took direct action against the Cardassians who had invaded this world and routed the—the inhabitants.

The handful of Cardassians and their Drek'la footsoldiers had struck upon the perfect tactic . . . The Natives, though not technological themselves, somehow had access to bucketsful of technological toys left over from a previous higher civilization. But everything worked off of broadcast power from central power plants relayed by local stations. The Cardassian-led assault teams simply blew up the relay stations, obliterating all power to a given region; and all the deadly toys used by the Natives instantly ceased operation, leaving them utterly defenseless, stunned, confused, ready to be harvested like scything wheat.

The captain's plan is bold, thought Worf; *it is Klingonlike. No other Starfleet officer would have dared!* Sisko had decided, after much agonizing, to take his team to the central power plants and knock them off-line himself, plunging the whole planet into darkness. The Natives, forced to react to the loss of power for weeks or months before the invaders got to them, would be over the shock and better able to resist conquest.

The only problem, however, was that the power plants were thousands of kilometers away . . . and the away team was on foot. They would need to find an enemy camp, somewhere, and liberate a skimmer to have any chance at all.

Worf, as usual, was first to express his opinion on the purely military question of tactics once they located the Cardassians. "I have nothing against stealth, Captain; as you know, Kahless himself often used stealth against a superior enemy—it is entirely honorable."

"For once," said Quark, "I *totally* agree with the wise commander."

"However," continued Worf, glaring at the Ferengi, "in this case, I do not think we can manage to steal a skimmer without being detected. We do not look anything like Cardassians or Drek'la."

"Oh, I don't know, Worf." The Klingon turned and immediately fell into a defensive posture: the speaker was a very mean-looking Cardassian wearing a face mask and the uniform of a gul. Worf grabbed the Cardassian infiltrator with one hand while he drew his *d'k tahg* knife with the other, but his brain finally caught up with his warrior's body, and he realized he was about to plunge a knife into the absent heart of Security Chief Odo.

"Odo!" he snarled. "You fool, I could have killed you!"

"Not unless your *d'k tahg* can penetrate a centimeter of titanium," replied the changeling laconically, tapping his breastplate.

"Odo makes a pretty compelling argument, if you ask me," said Chief O'Brien.

Taking a deep breath and calming his violent impulse, Worf decided it was honorable to admit when one was in error, despite the merriment that might give to the wretched Ferengi. A glare from the Klingon following the admission silenced Quark.

The captain smiled. "Odo has given us the seeds of an excellent plan. Now let's see if we can't make them grow into something tactically usable."

Lieutenant Commander Jadzia Dax quickly ran through a pro forma departure checklist with Julian Bashir; most of her mind was busy living anywhere but the present, crammed into a tight and motion-constricting dry suit, an air tank backpack, mask, and flippers within easy reach. The Nylex gloves made her palms itch, and the rolled up hood pressed uncomfortably against the back of her neck. *I'll bet Julian is as comfortable in Nylex as he is in a uniform,* she griped inwardly.

Her mind ranged ahead and behind, worrying about everything in the quadrant. She worried about Joson Wabak, the jaygee now in command of the submerged *Defiant;* she had issued final orders for him to follow another suggestion from the strangely helpful Julian Bashir: the seventeen-hundred-meter-tall antenna that would poke into the air.

Subspace communications between the ship and the surface had been swallowed up as soon as the planetary defenses spotted them; but perhaps they could still transmit along the surface. If not, both Julian and Jadzia had modified their combadges to send and receive in the radio frequencies of the electromagnetic spectrum . . . just in case. In either event, she would probably need line-of-sight with the raised antenna, unless they could bounce the radio signal off the cloud cover.

Jadzia fretted about the hull integrity of the ship, even though she herself had supervised the containment field modifications; if the hull began to buckle, Wabak would have to order them to upship and face Cardassian pounding again. She nervously wondered how long the runabout hull would withstand the ocean pressure; she was terrified of the possibility of having to scuba to the surface, despite two run-throughs in the holodecks with the good Dr. Bashir. And she still fumed about her performance in the battle, poor enough by her own standards that she had relieved *herself* of command.

Get a grip, girl, she commanded herself; *your mind is everywhere but here and now.* Julian finished the departure checklist and segued immediately into the launch checklist; Jadzia absently responded.

She touched all the right touchplates, slooshing with every flex of her dry suit, and got the engines spun up to speed; then she said, "Off the checklist, Julian; let's flood the launch bay."

She glanced at the doctor—always too cute by half to attract her; she liked her men rugged and perhaps a little cruel looking—and both of them took deep breaths as Jadzia pressed the transmit touchplate: *"Amazon II* to *Defiant;* open the floodgates, Joson."

"Aye, aye, Commander," said the Bajoran jaygee. Dax heard a loud bang, followed by a prolonged clanking; she imagined an immense anchor chain winding up somewhere, pulling open the locks to let the seawater rush into the bay. Looking out the front viewscreen, she rotated the fish-eye lens to show the hastily improvised "floodgate"; a stream of blue green water shot through the small holes, kicking up a turquoise froth as it poured across the deckplates and began to fill up the launch bay.

"I guess around here," said Julian, tugging at his own hood, rolled and circling his neck, "the Natives go *blue*-water rafting." Jadzia debated making a witty comeback, but decided the doctor's joke was feeble enough not to warrant response. *It's just his way of warding off anxiety,* she told herself.

Soon, the water was crashing around the runabout's legs, and in a few moments, climbing up high enough to start filling the viewscreen. After four minutes of flooding, Joson Wabak said, "Flooding complete; you're clear to launch. Good luck, Commander."

"Don't forget about the giant antenna," said Dax, "and don't hesitate to take off if you have to. You can probably leave orbit before the Cardassians spot you."

"Come on, Jadzia," said Bashir, "he knows what to do."

"And Joson. Listen on both subspace and radio frequencies for our signal . . . we might need you in a hurry."

"Aye, aye, Commander," said the Bajoran.

"Goodbye, Lieutenant," shouted Dr. Bashir, killing the com-link. "Jadzia, are you going to release the docking clamps? Or are we taking the *Defiant* with us?"

Jadzia Dax sighed and touched the release light. The ship shuddered and immediately began drifting towards the overhead; though she'd been somewhat expecting it—the ship was essentially an air bubble—the rapid movement still took her by surprise. By the time Dax corrected for the drift and brought the *Amazon II* under control, they were dangerously close to the ceiling.

"Dax to Wabak; open the launch bay doors." The doors slid open with a grinding noise, much louder than normal because the seawater conducted sound so well. The commander piloted the *Amazon II* perfectly through the dilated aperture and shot into the open ocean. Behind her, she knew, the doors were slowly contracting and the seawater being pumped out of the bilge. For good or ill, they were committed to their ocean adventure.

Ensign Joson Wabak tried desperately not to tremble under the crushing weight of sixteen hundred meters of seawater above him and a crew of seventy-eight below. *In command!* He was twenty-three years old, a newly minted ensign in Starfleet, and *in command* of the *U.S.S. Defiant.* It was an awesome and shuddersome thought. Command might have been intoxicating were they in orbit, instead of scuppered at the bottom of a purple sea.

"Containment shields down to forty-six percent," announced his erstwhile classmate, Ensign N'Kduk-Thag, or Ensign Nick, as Commander Dax had dubbed it, in its uninflected voice; unlike Vulcans, who experienced emotions but suppressed them (Joson had been told), the Erd'k'teedak literally did not experience emotions the way Bajorans like Ensign Wabak did. Under extreme stress, their rational centers might shut down, and they could begin acting what would be called mad were it any other race: Joson had personally seen N'Kduk-Thag marching naked in a circle around the flagpole at the Academy, chanting Starfleet general orders at the top of its lungs, in the middle of finals week one year. Joson steered his friend inside before the other cadets could see and misunderstand.

"Measurement of hull distortion up to one point three percent water seepage detected on outer hull behind containment shield alongside decks four through nine suggest ship is in danger of collapse."

Joson's mouth was dry. *How wonderful . . . my first command, and I to preside over the* Defiant *being crushed like an egg in a clenched fist!* 1,640 meters of seawater above them translated to about a hundred and sixty atmospheres of pressure on a hull never designed for more than one! Normally, the *Defiant* drifted through mostly empty space, bumping into only the tiniest wisps of hydrogen or the occasional micrometeor. In a pinch, the ship was also designed to plough its way into the atmosphere of a relatively Bajorlike planet, dealing with air pressure of perhaps as much as two atmospheres.

But the water pressure outside was more than eighty times that maximum rating. The only reason the ship wasn't already smashed to a mangled hulk of metal was that Commander Dax had personally modified the shields to strengthen the external containment surrounding the hull.

But not enough, thought Joson glumly. "Ensign Weymouth," he said, catching the attention of the third commissioned officer on the bridge; everyone else was a chief petty officer or below, and refused to make command decisions—though they often were overeager with advice.

"Yeah, Joss?"

Joson waited, frowning down at her from the command chair.

"I mean,—yes, sir?"

"Instrument check?" She was supposed to follow with a readout of all the pertinent instruments as soon as N'Kduk-Thag finished its readout of engineering diagnostics.

"Oh, sorry!" Stung from her contemplation of the forward viewer, whose image of the seafloor (color-corrected for water transparency) seemed to mesmerize her, Tina fluttered her hands over the combined navigation and science console. "Uh, uh, cloak is holding fine; nobody's detected us, I think—at least they haven't scanned us. Scanning around the ship; no, nothing but a big . . ." Weymouth's voice trailed off, and she stared bug-eyed at the scanner display.

"Ensign, what is it?" demanded Joson, feeling tentacles of fear wrap around his own head. *Just what I need, more trouble! Now what?* But Weymouth merely sputtered. *Blood of the Prophets, it's just like at the Academy!* Cadet Weymouth barely graduated at the bottom of the class; in fact, she had to repeat her first Academy cruise, because she "downed" it—received a failing mark from the instructor for freezing a several critical junctures. "Tina, *snap out of it!* What the hell do you see?"

"It's . . . it's huge! And it's coming this way!"

"*What's* huge? *What's* coming this way?"

Weymouth turned completely around in her seat

to stare at acting-Captain Wabak. "Joss . . . it's a sea monster!"

Both Wabak and N'Kduk-Thag stared at the girl. "By a sea monster do you mean a large aquatic creature?" asked Ensign N'Kduk-Thag.

"By a sea monster," snarled Weymouth, "I mean *this!*" She touched a light on her console and put the short-range scanner image on the forward viewer.

Joson Wabak stared at the shadowy, fluctuating image of a creature more than two kilometers in length, with thousands of hundred-meter tentacles waving about, and a gaping maw that was doubtless the thing's mouth. The "aquatic creature" was fifteen klicks away but moving fast enough to arrive within the half hour.

"N'Kduk-Thag," said Joson weakly, "could you please do a computer search through the Starfleet first-contact manual for any references to—ah—sea monsters?" The ensign-in-command was only half joking.

CHAPTER 3

"READ ME OUT the hull pressure and containment integrity, Julian; thirty second intervals."

"Aye, aye, Jadzia." The doctor unbuckled from his seat and slooshed to the midsection of the runabout, reading the strain gauges directly rather than trusting to the helm instruments; high pressure and strange minerals in the water might mess up the electronics, but the strain gauges themselves were so simple as to be virtually foolproof. "One hundred and sixty-two atmospheres on the outer hull," he said, "containment field integrity is . . . well, call it ninety-six percent. Looking good so far, Dax."

She checked her own instruments, and they differed from the gauges by only three or four percent, within expected tolerance at this depth. For the first time, she breathed a sigh of relief; *we might just make this without having to put our flippers on.*

With every ten meters they rose in the runabout-submarine, they bled off another atmosphere of pressure on the hull. Soon Julian was calling out "a hundred and fifty . . . hundred forty-nine . . ." Dax realized she was sweating; *it's just the suit,* she told herself. But the suit wouldn't explain her pounding heart and the fact that she caught herself clenching and unclenching her fist so much, her forearm started to ache.

"Pressure one forty," said the doctor, "containment integrity is—"

The suspense became unbearable. "Yes? Is what?"

"Well, I don't like the looks of this, Jadzia."

"What? What don't you like?" Dax started to breathe too quickly, to shallowly; she took a deep breath, forcibly calmed herself down.

"Well, it was holding nicely at ninety, ninety-one percent, but it just dropped to eighty-five in the last minute. Whoops, eighty; it's dropping fast, Jadzia. Can we ascend any faster?"

Dax pointed the *Amazon II* virtually nose-up and increased the thrusters as much as she dared; the ship was never intended to "fly" through water, just a single atmosphere or the vacuum of space. She couldn't push the engines any faster than the fraction necessary to move at ten meters per second.

"Wait," shouted Bashir; "pull back, slow down!"

Shaking, Dax cut engine power to nearly zero; vertical motion slowed to a crawl, one meter for every three seconds . . . *same speed a diver is supposed to ascend,* she remembered from the doctor's scuba instructions. "Julian, talk to me. What's going on?"

"It's the speed. The water drag is sapping the containment field; it's down to sixty percent . . . but the drop-off has slowed. We might still make it. Pressure one hundred atmospheres and falling."

Briefly, Jadzia Dax wished she were a Bajoran, so she could pray to the Prophets. Dry-mouthed, she increased the rate of ascent to balance field collapse with reduction of hull pressure.

Julian continued to call the numbers: "Hull ninety, field fifty-four percent; hull eighty, field fifty; hull seventy, field forty-five . . . we're going to make it, Dax."

"Yes we are, yes we're going to make it," she mumbled. Then she felt a drop of water on her forehead. Her breath caught in her throat; *it's just sweat,* she said, as it rolled down her face and into her mouth. It tasted of saltwater . . . but of course, sweat *was* saltwater. She spat it out, suddenly remembering the high cyanide content in the local flora.

But after several more seconds, she felt another drop, then a steady trickle of them. "Julian," she croaked, "we're leaking."

"Yes, here too," he confirmed. Jadzia risked a glance back; the thin, dapper doctor was actually holding his hand against the skin of the runabout, swiveling his head back and forth between the two main gauges. "Fifty atmospheres, thirty percent. Jadzia, pull your hood on and don mask and backpack; I'm going to start a controlled flooding of the cabin."

"You said we were going to make it," she said, trying to make light by clicking her tongue.

"We will," said Julian, with equally false *bon homie;* "but I didn't say the *Amazon II* would."

Dax said nothing more, just pulled on the rest of her scuba gear as quickly and efficiently as she could. By the time she finished, water was spraying into the cabin from every seam, and several of the instruments on her panel were giving obviously fractured readouts.

She pulled up her regulator, blew a few experimental blasts to clear it, and clamped her teeth around it. By the time she was ready, the water was above her waist. She looked at Bashir, and he gave her the scuba diver's "okay" circle of thumb and finger; Dax returned it, feeling nowhere near as okay as she put on.

Julian removed his regulator long enough to say, "It's going to be colder than the holodeck. Don't panic; just do it exactly as we practiced. I'll stay with you every meter, and I'm an expert diver, so don't worry."

Dax could barely hear him, and she felt a sharp pain in her ears. *Of course,* she realized; the air pressure inside the *Amazon II* was climbing. She held her nose and blew gently but firmly, clearing first one ear, then the other with a sharp pop.

The icy water touched her exposed chin; Julian was right . . . it was freezing. The rest of her body was comfortable in the insulated, electroheated suit, but she gasped at the coldness on her face and forgot to breathe for a moment. The water quickly filled the rest of the air pocket, and the runabout was entirely full of dark, turgid seawater.

Without worrying about her buoyancy compensator vest, she joined Julian at the emergency door crank; he opened the door slowly. Dax felt her ears plug up again; she checked her depth gauge, and realized that they were actually sinking. *Engines must've died,* she understood. Then Julian tugged at her arm, and she followed him out the partially opened door into the darkly luminescent, alien ocean.

The doctor reached across and pressed a button on Jadzia's chest; she seemed to shoot away from the runabout . . . but checking her gauge (which she could barely see, though it was lit) it was the other way around: she had come to a halt, while the *Amazon II* sank rapidly back toward the oblivion of the ocean floor. *That's it,* she thought; *we're on our own, for good or ill.* After several seconds, the lights from the runabout faded into the dark, murky depths.

She cleared her ears again, twisting her neck to stretch the Eustachian tubes. Then Bashir caught her attention and gave a thumbs-up—which in scuba signalling, she remembered, meant "Let's go up."

Dax felt another wave of panic: they were *fifty-five meters deep.* That was much deeper than even expert divers usually went, and Jadzia Dax was a rank amateur. She started to bolt for the surface, but Julian anticipated her misstep, and he caught her by the weight belt. She tried to kick him away, but she was hampered by the dry suit and the fluid water, and the doctor was a lithe and wily wrestler in any event. After several moments, she calmed down somewhat, though her pulse still pounded so loud, it shook her entire body with every beat.

Julian held up three fingers: "Three," he seemed to say, "three seconds per meter when ascending . . . no faster."

He started off in a thoroughly improbable direction—he was going the wrong way. Then Jadzia noticed the air bubbles expended from her regulator with every strangled exhalation went the same direction as Dr. Bashir. *Well, I might be confused, but I'm sure the damned bubbles know which way is up.* She followed the doctor, laboring to make each flipper stroke slow and cautious.

The darkness terrified her for some reason; she

had never been afraid of the dark before. But this wasn't just the absence of light; it was palpable, it reached out and enveloped her. She saw flashes of bioluminescent fish (or plants; she couldn't quite tell), but that only made the surrounding darkness seem lonelier and more solid. Her buoyancy compensator (BC) vented air automatically to maintain neutral buoyancy.

She continued to breathe, in and out. "If you hold your breath when you ascend," the good doctor had told her, "the compressed air can expand inside your lungs and force bubbles through your alveoli and capillaries into your bloodstream." Additionally, ascending too quickly caused the nitrogen gas in the diver's blood to come out of solution and form more bubbles. He went on to describe the symptoms of "the bends" *(rather gleefully,* thought Dax), and pointed out that the only known cure—putting the victim in a hyperbaric pressure tank and taking him "down" to the point where the gas bubbles dissolve into the bloodstream again, would be impossible on the surface of Sierra-Bravo 112-II (which did not, as far as they could tell, have any local hospital facilities).

Dax watched both her chronometer and pressure gauge. After a minute, they were still thirty-five meters deep, but the light was growing steadily stronger. Things were looking up. Then something brushed her leg . . . something *enormous.*

She didn't want to look down and see what it

was, but the image drew her eyes against her will. She saw the dim outline of something vaguely turtlelike, but at least twenty meters long: there was a hard shell, and dozens of flipperlike legs sticking out along the sides.

The monster swam into the darkness, and Jadzia gave a startled yelp into her regulator. She grabbed Bashir, pointing the direction it had vanished, but he evidently hadn't seen anything. He shook his head, pointing up.

They began to ascend again, but Jadzia Dax kept looking in every direction, hoping to spot it before it was too late. *So big deal, what good is that going to do? You don't want to be eaten without being instantly aware of it, eh?*

The monster turtle loomed out of the gloomy water directly in front of the pair, and this time there was no mistaking it by either party. The head suddenly filled Dax's entire field of view; or rather, *heads*—there were four of them, each with its own neck poking out from under the carapace.

First one then another head pressed close, opened its mouth, and unrolled a snakelike tongue with its own eyeball and set of needle teeth at the end. The tongue-mouths prodded at Dax and Bashir, feeling them, probably tasting them. Neither officer dared move. A pair of tongues wrapped around Jadzia and began pulling her closer to the mouth.

She reacted without thinking, reaching down to draw her dive knife and slashing at the only tongue she could reach. Julian saw what was happening and joined her, hacking at the same tongue as she; he grabbed it and began sawing back and forth.

Reacting sluggishly, the head the tongue was connected to finally uncoiled and jerked back; the head squirmed left and right, banging into the heads on either side: they appeared to forget their prey and turn on each other, and Dax immediately guessed that rather than being one monster turtle with four heads, she was looking at *four* turtles that shared the same shell.

As soon as it—they—let go, she almost bolted toward the surface, but she maintained adamantine control. They continued their slow ascent, and the monster turtles swam away, still bickering among themselves. By the time they faded from view, Jadzia Dax was shaking like a Trill *pacheepa* rat that had just escaped an owl.

A minute and a half later, the light suddenly got brighter and bluer; she saw the surface of the ocean above her head like a shimmering, undulating glass ceiling. Giant Sierra-Bravo kelp loomed in the distance to one side, and Dax guessed that was the direction of the ocean shelf they had mapped from the *Defiant;* after all, the kelp had to attach to something, and the trench into which the ship had settled was much too deep for such large plant life—not enough sunlight.

It was harder than ever for Jadzia to restrain

herself and not drive for the surface, glittering just fifteen meters above them; such a panicky dash could easily *kill her* in the absence of effective medical care. Gritting her teeth (and feeling phantom tongues nipping at her flippers), Jadzia ascended, if anything, even more slowly for the glass ceiling.

Jadzia Dax spit out her regulator, letting it fall back down by her side, but before she could get the snorkel into her mouth, a swell washed over her head, choking her. She bit down hard on the snorkel and did all her coughing into the mouthpiece; after a few moments, she was breathing without obstruction . . . her heart pounded, and she made a mental note for the doctor to examine her for cyanide poisoning.

Julian tapped her on the shoulder and removed his own snorkel for a moment. "Are you all right?"

She nodded, then shook her head, not wanting to talk.

"Ready to head for shore? It's that direction." He pointed toward the kelp, now visible as thin stalks that looked almost like celery rising two meters out of the ocean. Dax nodded again.

Julian unreeled a thin cord and connected them together; then he rolled onto his back, making sure Jadzia did the same, and activated the jets on their backpacks. They began to chug toward the shore at the stately pace of one kilometer per hour.

Jadzia just kept breathing in and out, with deep, slow breaths, trying to dispel the last remnants of her anxiety. Julian hooked his arm in hers to keep them close enough not to snag the tether on the alien kelp. By the time she began to see lots of bright-blue, four-legged fish swirling around her wake, she felt a bump against her feet; then realized it was a rock near the shore. Within a few more seconds, her heels were dragging in the silt, and she cut her motor at the same time Julian cut his.

"Well, Jadzia," he said brightly, "we seem to have arrived."

She smiled weakly, stripping off the dry-suit and submitting to a medical exam; the hard part was over . . . now all they had to do was find Benjamin and the away team somewhere in hundreds of square kilometers of trackless wasteland.

Julian Bashir hunched protectively over his friend, his comrade, his—*professionalism, professionalism.* Jadzia Dax was curled into a fetal ball, clenching her arms around her throbbing, aching belly. She had evidently swallowed a mouthful of the poisonous seawater at some point; *probably while on the surface,* thought the doctor, The seawater contained relatively high traces of cyanogene and radical cyanogens, which changed within the human (and Trill) body to a substance uncomfortably close to deadly cyanide. That she had only partially recovered from the battle wound she had recieved only days ago wouldn't help her condition.

Dax had evaded Cardassian ships and the planet's own automated defenses to plunge the *Defiant* deep into the deadly ocean waters. Communications with the away team were impossible through the electrolyte-laden water, and too dangerous to boot: if either Cardassian attackers or electronic planetary defenders intercepted the signal—well, it would take only a single concussion bomb to tip the balance, tear away the containment field, and allow the ship to be crushed beneath hundreds of atmospheres of pressure.

It was Dax's idea to replicate a long wire and send old-fashioned *radio waves* to communicate, but of course, there was no way for the away team to know what was required. So Dax, accompanied by the obvious candidate, the dashingly brilliant and resourceful chief medical officer, made a break for the surface in a runabout. They barely made it alive—*one more alive than the other,* thought Dr. Bashir, looking sadly at his patient, wondering whether she would make it. Now, dressed in replicated clothing similar to that of the native "Natives," they sat on the surface, grounded, one struggling to live, the other struggling against despair at his own helplessness to help.

From his emergency medikit, Bashir extracted his hypospray and reloaded another dose of the supposedly all-purpose antipoison supplied by the

Federation—and modified slightly by Dr. Bashir back aboard *Deep Space Nine.* He injected the antipoison and another muscle relaxant near her lungs (biggest concern) and her stomach (where most of the pain came from), and Jadzia relaxed as her pain eased. She was still unconscious from the sedative he had given her earlier; there was no reason for her to be awake to fight this mild poisoning.

"Correction," said the doctor aloud; "it's not *Deep Space Nine* any longer. It's . . ." What did the Kai say she was going to call it? *Oh yes, Emissary's Sanctuary.* Stupid name! But Bashir shrugged, trying to make the best of a life that always seemed balanced on one precipice or another. If he wasn't dreading possible exposure as a DNA-resequenced freak of unnature, he was being uprooted and probably split from all his friends and colleagues and sent to some forsaken hellhole—possibly to serve as the doctor on a Rigelian penal colony, perhaps, or worse, as personal physician to some pompous, overstuffed admiral nearing retirement.

What he really wanted, if he could no longer have his home on *DS9—Yes!* Deep Space Nine, *by no other name!*—would be a berth on a Galaxy-class starship, like the *Enterprise* that Miles had left to join the station (and Worf, too, remembered Bashir with a touch of a grimace, looking down at Jadzia).

"Modern medicine!" he derided; all he could do was ease her pain a bit and help her own body fight off the invasion of a toxic foreign substance. If she were going to survive—and he was now sure she would—it wouldn't be because of Dr. Julian Bashir, dashing lieutenant of Starfleet in the United Federation of Planets. Whether she lived or died had actually been determined however many years ago it was that Jadzia was conceived, when egg and sperm combined with a set of chromosomes that decided Jadzia's future resistance to infection, poison, and injury.

Though come to think on it, the symbiont Dax might also be helping against the poison. Not even the Trill themselves knew everything about the complex interactions between host body and symbiont.

Julian sighed. Modern medicine! Now he had much more precise and less invasive methods . . . so he could monitor his patient's own body desperately fighting off cyanide poisoning. Such progress! With a full laboratory, he might actually have been able to do something

But sitting on the sands of an alien seashore, staring at the deep, deadly ocean of violet waters full of poisons and four-headed monster turtles, lost on a planet already under invasion by Cardassian-led forces, caught in the gaze of who-knew-how-many dangerous native life-forms, helpless in the shadow of technology so vast, it practically dwarfed the Federation—but so fragile, the Cardassians could turn it off like a light panel on the *Defiant*—Julian Bashir felt like a child lost in a zoo in blackest night, knowing that all the cage doors were left open for the beasts to feed.

CHAPTER 4

JULIAN BASHIR jerked awake, groping wildly for his medikit. He had been dreaming that Dax was convulsing herself to death, dreaming he was asleep and dreaming, but unable to rouse himself from the dream *(in* the dream) to save her. He finally shouted himself awake and grabbed his kit . . . but Jadzia was nowhere about.

He stumbled this- and that-a-way, performing the "drunkard's walk" of a man just risen, thinking he had a terribly important task to perform but not remembering what. *Gods, what I wouldn't pay for a coffee just now,* he thought through a bleary cerebrum.

The first evidence of the missing lieutenant commander that Dr. Bashir found was a pair of boots that looked suspiciously like Dax's. Toiling up a nearby hilltop in the direction pointed by the shoes, dropped one then the other, he discovered her hooded robe. Shirt, pantaloons, and undergarments followed.

"What now, O mighty one?" the doctor asked Jadzia.

She shook her head. "The only obvious course is to head toward the original landing site. The away team doesn't have a vehicle, so they can't have got too far." She looked pensive. "Unless they commandeered something."

"From the Natives?"

"Natives? No, so far as we could tell, they'd never even heard of vehicles."

Bashir stared skeptically at the landscape, impossibly rich-blue mountains, brittle clouds, chill, white sun struggling up a vermillion sky. "This whole planet smacks of . . ."

"What?"

The word wouldn't come for a moment, elusively dancing just out of reach of the doctor's cerebrum, like the sweet odor that enticed his nostrils, or the metallic taste of latinum and other minerals and salts on his tongue. Suddenly, the word he sought ventured too close, and he reached out and snared it. "*Artificiality.* The way you described it, they have massive amounts of technology but no underlying infrastructure, and no scientific understanding whatsoever. Does that strike you as likely?" Julian was thinking of the implausibility of stone-age humans with hyposprays and medical scanners but without even the germ theory of disease.

"Well, I was thinking about that myself. If they're the degenerated descendants of an earlier, technological world—"

"Then there would be broken pieces of techno logical infrastructure all over the planet," finished Julian. "Roadways or launching ports or massive industrial structures. Not a bunch of high-tech stone huts and a random scattering of useful tools and weapons."

Dax sat down, chin in hand; her neck spots were dark, almost iridescent—*possibly a sign of intense thought,* figured Julian. "There would also be vehicles," said Dax, "either operative or crashed, and warp drive—you knew that some of the toys we found used elements of warp field technology, didn't you?"

"They did?" The doctor was surprised; he had been too busy with casualties to read all the reports the team sent up seemingly every few minutes. "Well, that's all the more reason the whole situation seems artificial!"

Dax looked up. "You're right, Julian. I think these people were *put here* by someone . . . and the entire planetary ecology was transplanted to feed them. The keepers, whoever they were, sprinkled the rock with enough toys that the Natives could play whatever games they wanted, but not enough for them to leave . . . or even travel around their own planet much."

"But there was never any struggle for survival," said Bashir quietly, finding the whole idea creepy to the point of being frightening, "and without that struggle . . ."

"They never developed a culture, a civilization, or any consciousness of groups larger than those who lived in the villages."

"The planned communities."

Dax chuckled. "So does that mean the experiment or whatever it was succeeded or failed?"

Bashir felt a shiver slowly crawl along his spine like a frozen centipede. "I wonder whether the Tiffnakis—is that what the villagers you met called themselves?—are even the same species as the rest of the Natives? Could they interbreed? Or have they been separated so long, they're no longer a single people?" The question seemed a natural to the doctor.

She shrugged, dismissing the speculation before Bashir could finish chewing on it. "Well, no matter. That makes the case stronger: the only way the away team could have a skimmer is if they borrowed one from the Cardassians. And my friend, dear Doctor Bashir, that is exactly what *we* are going to have to do."

Julian smirked—to hide his increasing nervousness, he realized. "You think they're going to be in a generous mood, our Cardassian friends? Or was one of your hosts a Drek'la and you remember the secret password?"

"No, but I'm sure if we ask them correctly, they

won't even miss it. Come on, Julian, start a slow, careful, long-range scan to find the nearest Cardassian military unit. I'll scan for ion trails left by the skimmers. Let's see just how far we're going to have to walk."

The sea monster—*we're all calling it that now,* thought Joson Wabak with a gulp—continued to approach the *Defiant* directly. There was now no question, as N'Kduk-Thag unemotionally informed him, that the monster had detected them somehow and was coming to investigate . . . or feed.

Heedless of how it would look to his "troops," who after all, were barely less-senior ensigns than he himself, Joson paced in front of the command chair, feeling anxiety creep on kitty feet around his stomach. He hadn't fought in the Resistance; he was too young when the Cardassians pulled out, and his mother wouldn't even entertain the idea of him trucking with the freedom fighters before then. Joson was uncomfortably aware that he had never been tested; the swordsmith had never struck him against the anvil to see which broke.

Well, neither has any other officer here! he thought defiantly—a thought that didn't comfort him, the more he considered it. "Ten minutes to contact do you have any orders," reported and asked N'Kduk-Thag, "Ensign Nick," as the beautiful but hard Commander Dax had nicknamed the sexless Erd'k'teedak, only the fourth of its species to graduate from the Academy (and only barely; its academics were not exactly stellar).

Well, Wabak, you'd better say something! "How's the containment shielding, Tina?"

Her own voice was nearly as uninflected as Ensign Nick's, but in her case, it was probably because she had resigned herself to death, thought the Bajoran. "Shields down to thirty-four percent and not holding."

"You diverted power from the engines—"

"From everything not necessary for life support," she reported gloomily. "We've got maybe thirty more minutes before we're crushed to death. So maybe we'll have time to be eaten alive by the sea monster first."

"That will be *enough* of that talk, Ensign Weymouth." Joson was pleased that he sounded more confident than he felt. "Prepare to launch from the ocean floor and head for the surface."

Weymouth turned to stare at him. "Joson! The structural stress of movement will crush the ship immediately!"

He stared back. "Better to die trying, *Ensign Weymouth,* than huddle here and wait for death to hunt *us.*" As he said the words, Joson Wabak felt an amazing sensation flood his senses: fear was stamped out like an old campfire; he felt the surge of excitement that his brother must have felt when he undertook his first mission for the Resistance . . . the one that got him captured by the Cardassians.

But Jaras SURVIVED! shouted a triumphant voice in Joson's head, *and the mission was a success, the entire Occupation Ministry of Justice was destroyed by three packed-photon bombs smuggled inside, and Jaras was one of the smugglers!* The thrill of being a Bajoran who had lived under the Occupation and seen it thrown off by his own people, the passion of knowing what he was doing was *right,* the certainty of command flooded the veins and arteries of Ensign Joson Wabak, and he knew then why he, not Tina and not N'Kduk-Thag, was chosen to command in Dax's absence.

"Launch the *Defiant,* Ensign," he commanded calmly. "Let's meet our giant friend face to face. If we're going to die, we'll die like Starfleet officers, not like a shellclaw being cracked open by a *sivass* worm!"

The command tone shocked Weymouth out of her torpor; shaking, she jumped to touch the lit squares on her panel and ramp the engines up to a hundred and four percent. The *Defiant* began to shudder as the landing pods shook loose from the silt into which they had sunk.

"May I suggest dropping cloak and powering up the shields? Better to take the chance of being detected by the Cardassian ships and defend ourselves in case the sea monster launches an attack."

"Excellent suggestion, Mr. N'Kduk-Thag." Joson waited, but the ensign didn't object to being called "mister," evidently not truly caring what gender was arbitrarily assigned. N'Kduk-Thag took the praise as authorization to proceed; the shields wouldn't protect against the horrendous pressure from the water, of course, but if the sea monster used electromagnetic or other means of attack, or even tried to ram them, it might save their hides. *Sure hope the spoon-heads have stopped looking for us,* thought Joson; strangely, he felt more nervous about the Cardassians than about the more immediate dangers of sea pressure and the monster. He shrugged; *tradition, I suppose.*

The *Defiant* rolled peculiarly as they cruised forward, and Ensign Weymouth expressed repeated frustration at her lack of full helm control. "We are in the water one should expect a certain loss of attitude control," remarked Nick; Tina didn't seem pleased at the unasked for lecture.

"Can you search ahead with the sensors, N'Kduk-Thag?" asked Joson; "look for strong currents that might push us into an underwater mountain."

"Aye, aye sir."

"Tina, tie your helm viewer into Nick's sensors; set it up so the currents are color-coded by intensity." When the junior ensigns carried out their task, the ship's motion smoothed out; Weymouth was able to dodge the strongest currents as if navigating down a *bickett* warren. Still, Joson Wabak felt a peculiar, hollow feeling in his stomach, and his mouth grew dry; it took him several moments to diagnose himself: *Seasickness! I'm getting seasick. How wonderful.* He had known he was subject to the nausea and dizziness ever since he and his brother went out fishing in choppy waters one day, but it had never occurred to him that he would suffer from motion sickness in a modern-day starship. The inertial dampers were doing their job . . . Joson was being nauseated by the visuals through the forward viewer.

"Creature constant bearing decreasing distance contact in three minutes," reported N'Kduk-Thag. The ensign helpfully called out every thirty seconds, then counted down the final thirty.

"Is it stopping, Nick?"

"No, sir. Should we halt engines?"

"Not until it does!"

Tina gritted her teeth. "Oh m'God," she breathed, "we're playing *chicken* with a sea monster?"

The Bajoran ensign had no idea why Weymouth was talking about chickens, so he ignored the question. "Hold your course and speed."

"Thirty seconds twenty-nine eight seven six . . ."

"Sir!"

"Hold course."

"Twenty nineteen eighteen—"

"Joson, for God's sake!"

"Eleven ten nine . . ." Ensign Nick suddenly stopped speaking. "The creature has stopped contact in twenty-two seconds beep at current rate of closure."

Twenty-two seconds from the beep, I suppose. "Weymouth, wait ten seconds, then all stop." *YES!*

Wabak grinned, pleased to have won the first round. *But only the first round,* warned a little voice in his head.

The *Defiant* pulled to a stop, much more quickly than it would have in empty space, of course, because of water friction. The two entities faced each other: the Federation starship, fully armed but crippled under the pressure of more than a thousand meters of water still above them—and the amoeboid sea monster two kilometers long with thousands of vicious-looking tentacles just waiting to scoop up the bite-sized morsel and shove it into the creature's mouth.

"Let's get a good look at the thing, shall we?" said Joson, without the shakiness he actually felt. "N'Kduk-Thag, launch a probe across the monster's bow, have it circle around and get a good holo from every angle."

"Aye aye sir." Nick reached across to the empty science officer's console and touched a few lit squares; in the main viewer, Wabak watched the tiny probe streak away from the ship. The hundreds of tentacles nearby rippled with the probe's bow wave, and the ripple passed along the creature's body as the probe circumnavigated it, but there was no other reaction from the monster, which continued to regard the *Defiant* motionlessly. The ripples created a gentle, pink current, which the viewer still obligingly displayed. "I don't think it can see something as small as the probe," ventured Ensign Wabak.

Just as he finished the observation, and the probe rounded the back of the sea monster and headed back toward the ship, a pair of the tentacles uncoiled and lashed out, grabbing the probe as it streaked past. The force of the probe's momentum actually tore off one tentacle, but the other held fast, dragging the probe, despite its impulse engines, into the maw of the monster.

Fascinated, the three officers and two security petty officers on the bridge stared at the probe's visual transmission: they watched in awe as the probe was caught by hundreds of thousands of headless serpents or worms; Joson realized with a shock that they were *tongues,* each the size of a tree trunk! The tongues acted like teeth, pulling the probe apart and forcing the pieces down the gullet. After three minutes of wormy mastication, one of the tongues got hold of some vital piece of electronics, and the probe ceased to transmit.

"Tell me about the biology of the monster," said the ensign-in-command, trying to wrench everyone's attention back to the crisis. "Oh, and Weymouth—how's the hull integrity holding out?"

"Hull integrity not dropping as fast," said Tina, cutting off N'Kduk-Thag. "It's down to thirty percent, dropping one point every minute and a half, now that we're not so deep."

Silence. "*Defiant* to Nick, hello?" asked Joson.

"If you are ready to hear my report."

"Yes, N'Kduk-Thag; we are ready to hear your report." For all that Erd'k'teedak insisted they experienced no emotions whatsoever, they were well known to get miffed now and then . . . in a distant, intellectual sort of way. Weymouth's report had been the more important, but Nick was still irritated that she had cut him off.

"The probe sensors detected meter-thick muscle striations coiled with veins filled with latinum—"

"Latinum!"

"—that would doubtless impede photon torpedo penetration and of course the heavy mineral and electrolyte concentration in the seawater would interfere with the phasers in my judgment we have little chance of damaging the sea monster in combat."

"Thank you, Nick," said Tiny angrily, "that was worth waiting for."

Joson abruptly stood again, but stopped himself from pacing. *Think, think, think! What would Sisko do?* "I need options, people. How about a tractor beam? Can we push it away? Or push ourselves away from it?"

Nick played with his console. "No, sir. The seawater disrupts the beam as it would a phaser."

"Joson—I mean, sir, why don't we start ascending very slowly? Maybe we can at least reduce the pressure on the ship so we don't drown while this thing is making up its mind whether to eat us."

Damn! I should have thought of that! "Do it, Weymouth."

The internal com-system chirped. "Engineering to bridge," said a disembodied voice that Joson vaguely recognized from the watches he had stood down there.

"Wabak," he said absently.

"Sir, Lieutenant Abdaba here. We finished replicating that floatable antenna the commander ordered. Deploy?"

And may the Prophets ensure that neither the planetary sensors nor the spoon heads will think to check the electromagnetic spectrum for low-tech radio broadcasts, breathed Joson Wabak silently. The ionized salts and heavy metals suspended in the deadly ocean waters would prevent sensors from picking up the *Defiant,* especially at such a depth, but the tip of the antenna would necessarily have to be "hot," and in a radio-source scan, would stand out like a magnesium flare in a midnight marsh.

Licking his lips, the Bajoran ensign continued. "Nick, as soon as the antenna clears the shields, I want you to start transmitting on the radio frequencies of the EM spectrum—get me in contact with Commander Dax!"

"Aye, aye, sir."

"Sir, we're ascending at one meter per second; I'm hoping that's so slow we won't attract the monster's attention."

"Excellent, Tina. Keep a weather eye peeled." It was one of the few human expressions he had learned, but he couldn't tell whether Weymouth understood it. *Maybe she's from a different village on Earth,* he thought.

Three tense minutes ticked slowly by on the ship's chronometer; the *Defiant* had risen slightly less than two hundred meters, and now they were even with the center of the sea monster's squirming mass of tongues. Several flicked out to touch—*taste?*—the ship, but didn't get through the shields. Then suddenly, with no warning whatsoever, more than thirty tentacles lashed out and wrapped themselves around the ship, wrenching it to a halt and hurling Wabak to his hands and knees before the gravitic stabilizers could adjust.

"Damn it!" he blurted, then caught hold of himself and stood, lowering himself with dignity back into his command chair. "Damage report, Nick?"

"There is no damage. We have been brought to a halt. All upward motion terminated. The impulse engines are unable to break us free of the creature's grip. I am still transmitting but there has been no response from the secondary away team."

"Okay, this is it," said Joson, feeling a horrible sense of peace and calm permeate his body. "If that thing pulls us toward its mouth, we open fire with everything, and to *hell* with latinum muscles and electrolytes in the barbarous water."

Just then, Tina gasped. She half stood, staring down at her sensor display. "Joson!"

"Ensign, what is it?"

She stared wildly back and forth from Wabak to N'Kduk-Thag. "Nick's wrong, sir; there *is* a response to our transmission."

"Dax? You have Commander Dax? Patch her through!"

"No sir," said Ensign Weymouth, turning distinctly pale, "the response isn't from the commander."

"Then who's responding?" asked Joson, feeling his preternatural calm vanish in a rush of adrenaline. He knew what her answer would be a fraction of a second before she said it.

"She is," said Tina, pointing at the cavernous, serpent-toothed mouth that filled the entire forward viewer. "She wants to know where our mother is."

I wouldn't mind knowing that myself, thought Joson at first; his next thought was, *by the Prophets, I wonder how they're going to write THIS one up in my fitness report?*

CHAPTER 5

WITH GREAT MISGIVINGS, Captain Benjamin Sisko had left the Tiffnakis four days behind. *I want to stay and train them, train them some more, keep training them until they can overwhelm the invaders like fire ants pulling down a sunbathing lizard!* But he knew it would be an unconscionable waste of his time: Asta-ha—the hereditary mayor who had misunderstood the military ranks that Worf had taught her and had dubbed herself "Mayor-General"—was capable all on her own of turning the remaining two hundred Tiffnakis into soldiers; she had the help of her commando squad, the "Terrors of Tiffnaki," whom Sisko and his away team had finally shocked into recognizing reality . . . and into recovering their lost legacy of intelligence, creativity, and tactical thinking.

She wouldn't do as good a job as the captain and Worf could, and it would take longer. But there was a more urgent task for the away team: they had to knock *every power generator on the planet* off-line. Only in this way could the rest of the Natives on Sierra-Bravo be forced to confront real life . . . life without the toys that had been their source for everything they needed. Otherwise, the invaders would continue moving from village to village, cutting the local power and overwhelming the Natives while they were still in shock from the loss of their entire, "new tech"–driven world.

With one stroke, we can shatter their dream, thought the captain; *they will wake up—because they HAVE TO wake up. By the time the Cardassians meet them, weeks will have passed for them to get used to life without the Power.* Visions of bow- and spear-armed Natives ambushing Cardassians, who shot back with disruptors and concussion bombs, polluted Sisko's thoughts; it was a horrible, ugly sight . . . but not as ugly as the vision he had seen in reality: Cardassians mowing down abruptly *un*-armed Tiffnakis like a farmer scything wheat.

Sisko closed his eyes against the burning, orange sun: *Please,* he prayed—perhaps to the Prophets, since he was still the Emissary—*please, this time, let me be right!* The other possibility, as Chief O'Brien had cheerfully pointed out, was that knocking all the power off-line would result in mass starvation, death by exposure, and a quick and craven surrender to the Cardassians by the few remaining survivors. *Well, somebody has to find the dark lining, I suppose,* and it always seemed to be the chief, for some reason.

For four days, the away team had made excellent time. The toys that Sisko had forbidden to the Tiffnaki commandos and confiscated off their persons came in handy to smooth out the trail the Federation crew followed: the force beam flattened a path through scrub; the antigravs got them up and down cliffs; and the death rays worked wonders in cutting down small blue trees for bridges across rushing, metal-sparkling rivers whose waters were deadly to anybody but the Natives.

But in four days, despite the advantages, the team had made only sixty kilometers, a remarkable showing but not enough, not nearly fast enough! At the moment, they sat atop a bluff overlooking a deathly hot valley of bright, latinum-laced sand they would have to cross—all sixty klicks of it—and they were already running lower in com-rats than Sisko had estimated.

O'Brien sat on the edge of the cliff, dangling his legs over and staring bleakly at the wasteland below. Quark paced round and round a circle, mumbling to himself something that sounded suspiciously like "latinum, latinum everywhere, nor any strip to spend." *If Coleridge were alive today, he'd be spinning in his grave,* thought the captain mirthlessly.

Odo was a puddle, far away and secluded from the rest of the team; they had stopped ostensibly because the changeling had stayed too long in a solid state and was desperate to collapse and liquify. But Sisko knew the rest of the away team, himself included, were grateful for the chance to rest a complete day, sleeping as they could in the bright sunlight, readying themselves for the three-night trek across the desert.

The captain himself sat cross-legged on the bluff, by choice too far from the edge to see the sands below, squinting against the sun as it crawled in the direction they had arbitrarily labeled west. "Worf," he said, his first word in an hour.

The sleeping Klingon rose grunting, looking about to see who had called him from dreams of siege and liege. Sisko repeated the soft command, and Commander Worf struggled to his feet, joining the captain. "Yes, sir?"

"Worf, we are still a hundred and forty kilometers from the Cardassian landing spot, and sixty of those kilometers are across *that.*" Sisko nodded past O'Brien toward the cliff and the sands below.

"Yes, I am aware of that fact, sir."

"You are quartermaster. How many days rations do we have left?"

Worf worked his face, reluctant to answer. "Four days if we stretch it, Captain."

"And how long would you estimate it will take us to reach the launch facility?"

Worf said nothing; Sisko continued the narrative himself, wishing he had another answer. "Three days across the desert, if we're lucky; then Kahless knows how long to cross that mountain range. At this rate, Commander, we're not going to make it, are we?"

Worf stopped figiting. "No. We are not."

"And the damned invaders are going to win." Worf didn't speak; Sisko waited a beat, then turned to his real purpose. "Worf, you know all the legends and histories of the ancient Klingon wars, don't you?"

"I would not say all, sir; I do know a great many."

"We need that expertise now, Worf. Think, think! How would Kahless have gotten us to the enemy before our food ran out?"

Lieutenant Commander Worf stood, folding his arms sternly, staring at the horizon, the distant mountains they eventually would have to cross. "Even the Emperor Kahless had mechanized armor," mumbled the Klingon petulantly.

"Then think back farther! Think of the age of heroes, before any of the technology we take so much for granted. How the hell did they move armies around in those days?"

Worf turned back to Captain Sisko. "We used pack animals, of course. Riding beasts, and beasts to carry the gear."

Sisko nodded; it was the germ of a thought that had been scratching at his own forebrain for days . . . Worf had pulled it into the open so Sisko could finally examine it. "Yes . . . yes! That's it, that's what we're missing. If we were a *cavalry* unit, we might actually be able to make a hundred and twenty kilometers in four days . . . especially since we could feed and water the horses on native grass and native water!"

O'Brien had turned around during the conversation; now he said in excitement, "Captain! I think I've seen creatures here that might make almost adequate horses!"

"Which animals are you talking about?"

O'Brien stretched his arms to indicate great size. "They're huge beasties, they've got six legs and *I think* some kind of fur, unless it's needles. Their heads are kind of split down the middle, so they look like a double-barreled phaser?"

"Those giant six-leggers?" asked the captain, picturing the terrifying beasts in his mind. "Can they be domesticated?"

"Beggin' your pardon, sir, but do we have any choice?"

The Ferengi abruptly ceased his pacing and stared back and forth among the other participants in the conversation. "Have you people *lost your minds?* You expect me to ride on top of some hideous, two-headed, six-legged monster for hundreds and hundreds of kilometers? You're insane!

Forget it!" His fear was so palpable that Sisko almost felt sorry for the little fellow.

Almost. But there really was no other option. "Quark, you're just going to have to deal with it!" snapped O'Brien, saying essentially what the captain had been about to say—but a lot less diplomatically.

Worf grinned wolfishly. "I am sure the captain would allow you to stay behind—and leave your combat rations to the rest of us." Quark snorted indignantly and turned his back on the Klingon . . . something he never would have done had the two of them been alone in a dark corner of the station.

"Gentlemen," said Captain Sisko, "I believe we have a plan: Chief, you'd better get busy."

"Me? Doing what?"

"You've got a couple more hours before Odo rejoins us . . . and I want you to become an *expert* in lassoing wild monsters."

The explosion from the chief was enough to keep the captain amused for more than half an hour, by the end of which O'Brien was furiously hurling a loop of rope from the survival packs the *Defiant* beamed down; he hurled the loop at a tree trunk that Worf held aloft with the antigravity device—the method the pair had settled upon for lassoing the local "horses." *Next couple hours of training is going to be absolutely RIVETING,* decided Benjamin Sisko.

* * *

Kai Winn woke suddenly in the night. She sat bolt upright in bed, listening for the noise that had shaken her from her memories; but it was elusively absent. Her heart raced . . . at first, it was all she could concentrate upon, for the doctors had warned her that she very much needed to keep herself calm if she didn't want another "coronary incident," as they euphemistically put it. *No, no,* she warned herself; *that's not the way to do it!*

Instead, the Kai commenced a prayer to the Prophets, a child's exercise, actually; she recited the first syllable, then the first two, then the first three, and so forth, finally reciting the prayer song in its entirety on the thirty-third repetition . . . then repeated. It worked to slow her heart, but her nerves still jangled like an iron bell suspended in a stiff breeze.

"Kai Winn to Major Kira," she said.

"Kira—Kai, either come take command or leave me alone! We're in the middle of a fire fight here!" In the background, Winn heard the shout of orders, damage reports, too indistinct to make out over the com-link. She briefly considered rising, but she was dead tired . . . and if the station were in imminent danger of being lost, Kira would have awakened her.

"Are we holding our own, child?"

"Yes, damn it! I sent out the militia in pressure suits and it's hand to hand. Well, phaser to disruptor between *DS-Nine*—I mean, *Emissary's Sanctu-*

ary and the alien ships. We still don't know who they are. Now *please,* my Kai, clear the line so I can direct the fight!"

"I trust you, child. Awaken me in two hours or immediately if there is a breach."

"Aye, aye, Kai. Kira out." The major rudely cut the link herself, but Winn forgave her young protege; Nerys had much to learn . . . and she was learning even now. Calm patience was the priceless gift of the Prophets.

The Kai rose, pushing her pudgy feet firmly into the slippers she had owned since—well, since she was a sister in service to her "master," Gul Ragat. She walked to the shelf that used to contain a stack of Starfleet manuals on data clips when the Kai's quarters used to be the Emissary's office. Now the shelf had an infinitely higher purpose: it supported a large, nondescript box with a split front, a front the Kai touched reverently.

I must never turn to Them for trivial or personal matters, she thought to herself, as if once again lecturing in a religious school, a task she had not performed for many, many years. *This is not a personal matter,* she told herself firmly, *and this is no trivial question. The survival of Bajor may be at stake!*

Nervously, fearing that she may have everything all wrong and could be offending the Prophets, Kai Winn took a deep breath and opened the doors wide. The Orb was so brilliant, it burned right through her eyes, searing the back of her skull. She grimaced; she was, after all, a middle-aged woman—no longer in her physical prime, and not the Emissary. But she was the Kai; and the Prophets, though they burned and battered, had never failed their people.

"Show me," she whispered against the light, "show me Your will. Show me what I must know!"

Shocked, Winn found herself not looking into the minds or hearts of the enemies still attacking the station, not at the Federation or the Dominion, not even in her own time; she found herself back in the selfsame dream from which she had lately escaped by a panicked leap into consciousness. The Prophets wanted her to remember; the Prophets wanted her past. *I will give it to Them,* she yielded.

It made no sense to Kai Winn. But then, did it need to?

CHAPTER 6

THIRTY YEARS AGO

THE CARAVAN of Gul Ragat assembled in the courtyard outside the keep of the palace that once belonged to the town of Shiistir and served as the home of ex-Governor Riasha Lyas; now, the same building of light and color sheltered the conscience and the ears of Legate Migar from the lamentations of Sister Winn's people. *What a shock,* thought the priestess, *that the stone walls of this bloody place don't tumble to the earth in horror at what they've seen!* They looked as solid as ever, ready to stand for centuries of tyranny or freedom, uncaring, pink and cold as stone.

The outer wall was retained, but it was largely ceremonial; the protective function was taken by a force shield the Cardassians had erected, since they (unlike poor Lyas) had much to fear from assassins and saboteurs. The interior wall was shaped like a pair of octagons connected by a wide, rectangular *circus maximus* used for the bloody sports of the current masters—blood games that remained barbaric, no matter how refined and decadent the rules. *I cannot understand why the Prophets have not crushed this place!* she screamed to herself.

Sister Winn was the only cleric among the Bajoran mass of Gul Ragat's household; she had no idea whether she had a religious counterpart among the Cardassians . . . in fact, she wasn't even sure whether they even had a religion beyond worship of the state. If there were a Cardassian holy man or woman, he had not seen fit to knock elbows with the Bajorans. Among the gul's Cardassian retinue were two majors and his captain of the guard (one Colonel Baek); sixteen sergeants and soldiers astride individual skimmers; Neemak Counselor, the gul's personal secretary and attorney; a brutish Cardassian valet, Gavak-Gavak Das, who oversaw the Bajoran servants (Sister Winn's immediate boss, except that Gul Ragat had taken a liking to her, and she generally reported directly to the gul himself); Ragat's skimmer pilot; and a pair of mechanics/secretaries operating under the command of Neemak Counselor.

Gul Ragat also traveled with his household staff of Bajorans, numbering forty-two, including Sister Winn . . . who should have been considered the "slave overseer," since she was the nearest thing to an authority figure; but she eschewed the job, claiming a complete lack of "command presence," and Hersaaka Toos, a luckless impulse engine repair-crew foreman was given the task.

No command presence! The reality was that Sister Winn was already looking ahead to the days when Cardassia would be expelled from Bajor; she had seen the vision in her dreams, the coming of the Emissary, the intervention of the Prophets—and very frankly, she wanted a place guiding the destiny of her people when they were free. Politically, Sister Winn could never allow even a hint that she might have collaborated with the Cardassians; it would spell the death of her personal ambitions.

Winn was supposed to report with the others at zero-eight hundred (Cardassians were enamored of military time), but she had a guess how long it would take old Gavak-Gavak and Hersaaka Toos to muster sixty-five people in some semblance of order to satisfy the farewell inspection by Legate Migar and Gul Dukat; she wandered onto the scene a half hour late and stepped into her place, and she was not the last.

The contrast between the twenty-five Cardassians and the forty-two Bajorans was remarkable, though hardly worth remarking: Cardassians mustered at attention because they were a proud race of lordly conquerers who had yet to suffer any significant defeat in their drive to expand the Empire to Hell and back; the Bajorans stood glumly still in the cold wind because they didn't want to be lashed by Gavak-Gavak Das, who enjoyed his work all too thoroughly.

Still, even when squat Gavak-Gavak expertly flicked his whip end to graze the priestess's cheek, stinging but not drawing blood this time, she found herself hating him far less than she hated and *despised* the kindly, thoughtful Gul Ragat! "At least Das is an honest racist," she had told a divinity student three years earlier, when he passed briefly through Ragat's household. "Das is a brutal beast and he expects us to hate him for it. But the gul wants not just our obedience but our *love."*

"That's worse?"

"He oppresses us, child, but he bears false witness against himself, absolving himself of the charge of slavery by being a nice old slavemaster! His is infinitely the greater evil in the eyes of the Prophets." The student never quite got it; Sister Winn was saddened to hear that he was caught raiding the next year and was hanged.

When Gul Ragat and sixty-five lesser mortals were finally mustered under the chilly, gray sky, Old Migar and cold-eyed Dukat inspected them. Migar cared only for the ritual; it was power-hungry Dukat, the master of *Terok Nor,* orbiting Bajor like the grim hand of contagion (for wherever its shadow fell was death), who pulled Cardassians and Bajorans alike out of line and set them to perform brutal physical exercise in the frozen, muddy courtyard for such heinous crimes as unpolished boots, misaligned buttons, or "a surly attitude." The gul had one eye on the prefecture of all Bajor and the other on the advancing age and retirement (or sudden death) of Legate Migar, which still left him the eyes in the back of his head to spot treacherous malingerers and slackers. Even Gul Dukat, however, passed lightly over Sister Winn; he knew her to be her "master's" favorite, and as the saying went, Rank Hath Its Privileges.

Eventually, even Dukat was satisfied with the shininess of the glittering, silver filligree across the doublets of deepest military purple, with the velvet-red uniforms of the servants, and with the polish on the personal skimmers and armaments of the soldiery, little though they could shine on such a gloom day; and he passed in quick review one more time before vanishing back inside the house—to the banquet and open bar that Winn knew awaited him there. Migar sighed and followed Dukat, who technically outranked the governor, and at last, Gul Ragat could breathe in relief again and order Gavak-Gavak to get the splendid column moving—theoretically toward the village of Vir-Hakar in Belshakarri, their home . . . but in reality, on the road to Riis—*where all threads of this tapestry shall join,* thought Sister Winn.

CHAPTER 7

WINN THOUGHT she knew the route that Gul Ragat would follow; there was one obvious road from the palace to the river and Riis: along Surface 92, as the Cardassians called it. The Bajorans had a more colorful name: the Way of Wallows, because of the soft, marshy ground surrounding the road that in ancient times had been used to wallow *ttraks* being driven to the slaughter pens in Riis; there were slaughter pens no longer in peaceful Riis, but the road to the city founded three millennia ago by the holy man Kilikarri remained. Sister Winn had followed the road many times, though usually at many kilometers per hour skimming two or twenty meters above the ground, and she visualized the entire road in her mind, trying to figure the best place to desert.

She knew her holos were much more important than a single action in Riis, a few cell leaders who could not betray the Resistance even if they wanted—and the Cardassians could, of course, *make them* want—because of the elaborate organization of cutouts and false fronts; for all that, Winn found herself unable to condemn her fellow freedom fighters to capture, torture, and death, no matter what the cause. There were others, even other priests—Vedek Opaka sprang to mind—who were much more ruthless than she, and she knew, intellectually, it was a failing. *But I just can't do it!* she railed. She had to find a way to warn the Riis cell to call off the raid.

Her best chance would come during the second half of the march; Surface 92, which the Cardassians had straightened, now ran directly over the wallows across a series of high, arched bridges, some rising fifty meters above the surface. But there were places where the drop was only ten meters into soft mud, and Sister Winn decided that even she, not the most athletic of women, could survive that.

But then what? she pondered; getting off the road without being spotted was the easy part; traversing kilometers of slick, deep mud and swampy, stagnant lakes on foot would be the real test. She knew of a swamper, Velda Reeks, who was friendly to the Resistance; the woman had hidden fugitives before. But she lived four kilometers from the road . . . and those would be four kilometers of ghastly effort and terrible risk: if Gul Ragat missed her and thought to scan the surrounding swamp before she made it to Velda's shielded cabin, he would spot her in an instant and send soldiers to pick her up. She would be searched, the holos found . . . and not only would she be executed, but the cell at Riis would be thoroughly compromised, and perhaps even Velda Reeks to boot!

Sister Winn would have to be over the wall, into the mud, and away for several hours before anyone noticed she was missing; that meant a night escape, of course . . . but where would the gul decide to camp? He was restricted to the foot speed of the Bajorans, since no Cardassian in his right mind would leave his servants behind and rush on ahead; thus, it would take three days to get to Riis, which waited like an open hand upon the Shakiristi and its tributaries. But would they camp near enough to Velda's cabin that Winn could make it, assuming everything else went well?

She thought of one more stratagem: if she somehow could get into a skimmer, she might be able to program it to head out over the swamp in some other direction; then, when she turned up absent, the Cardassians would assume she had stolen the vehicle and would waste time following it. That might confuse them enough that they would never institute a thorough search that might uncover Velda's cabin.

The road to Riis was painful; there was no grassy median, as had been the case when it was a small Bajoran road, because Cardassians never traveled by foot; Surface 92 was constructed of a specially hardened plastic that could withstand the wheeled and tracked vehicles the Cardassians used for trucking heavy military equipment where antigravs were unavailable or not powerful enough. Winn wore only household shoes, and her feet were rubbed raw within the first few kilometers.

She had never walked so far without a rest. The gul was anxious to get to Riis before the uprising that only he knew about, and he drove his household mercilessly. Coming to the bulletin-tea was much easier; there was no rush, and they made only eight or nine kilometers per day, with plenty of time to sit and eat, sip refreshments, and otherwise "bathe their toes," as the saying went. Now, Gul Ragat pushed for twice that pace, and Sister Winn grimaced with every step.

Others were hardened to the pace, having lived rougher lives than the priestess; she didn't allow herself to complain, since she only suffered because she *hadn't* suffered as much as the others! But the blisters were real, and her pain was hard to bear. Only Winn's incessant prayers to the Prophets allowed her to endure that first day.

In the first of the two nights they would spend on the road, she showed her feet to Hersaaka Toos, and he sucked in a breath through clenched teeth; they did look ghastly. He sent her to the healer,

Daana, who prescribed balms and a foot wrap that soothed much of the pain and allowed the priestess to walk relatively normally again. Already, however, the whole "survival-evasion-resistance-escape" scenario was smelling less exciting and more implausible.

While the Bajorans set up the gul's camp, Sister Winn cased the field in the guise of hearing confessions and administering prayer and penance. Cardassian camps were uniform, and it was a matter of pride within Gul Ragat that *his* camp would break not the slightest letter of the law or breath of tradition. The night's camp centered around the manor of an unfortunate Bajoran farmer, who had stupidly chosen to live alongside a trade route and foolishly built up a successful farm: Mr. Farmer and his family were temporarily exiled to a small inn thirty kilometers away, driven in the gul's personal skimmer, while the entourage of Gul Ragat began pitching tents on one of the farmer's fields.

In an effort to be nice about it, the gul ignorantly picked a field that looked empty, but in reality, it was newly planted, a fact not brought to Gul Ragat's attention for half an hour and the significance of which took him another half hour to understand. By the time he moved the camp, the newly planted seeds were trampled and scattered; if they grew at all, they would grow haphazardly, not in rows, and be almost impossible to weed and water properly. Winn spent the time wincing and desperately praying to the Prophets that the farmer wouldn't be completely ruined, as so many others had been.

Gul Ragat situated himself in the main house, of course, and his soldiers pitched tents in orderly rows upon a field that had been ploughed but not yet planted; it would have to be reploughed, but that was only a matter of a few extra days work for the owner. The Bajoran servants were a special concern of Gul Ragat's; he worried constantly that they, too, were well weeded and watered. In consequence, he ordered Gavak-Gavak Das to house the Bajorans in the livestock barns . . . which the overseer promptly did by turning out all the stock and chasing it away.

"Ah, they'll come back, you whining priestess!" snarled Gavak-Gavak to Sister Winn when she protested. Winn stared after the departing rumps and hooves; true, the farmer would probably be able to get most of his dairy herd back again, but at what cost? It would probably take weeks to round them all up and truck them back to the farm!

The farmer's land—Winn never did find out the man's name—was at the edge of the mud flats, the Wallows; for the next two days, Surface 92 traversed a causeway . . . and the cabin of Velda Reeks was just about halfway between the farmer's hold and Riis. *Please, please,* prayed the priestess fervently, *let us stop tomorrow night near enough that I can at least try!*

Winn slept fitfully that night. Not only was she unused to camping out—she hadn't slept well on the road to Legate Migar's palace either—and not only could she not tolerate the dirty smell of animals, which permeated every cranny and crevice of the barn like a miasma, along with much animal by-product; but worst of all, she felt more strongly than usual the restless ghosts of Bajorans slain by evil Cardassians, by faceless bureaucracy, and especially by well-meaning apologists like Gul Ragat. She felt surrounded by the indifferent efficiency of the Cardassian soldiers, who joked about the inhumanity of the Bajorans without the least concern for the Bajorans at their backs, who outnumbered them almost three to one! And of course, no Bajoran servant dared even raise an angry glance at a Cardassian, lest he be made an example for the rest.

Hersaaka Toos, the Bajoran foreman, seemed the most oppressed by the burden of serving his planet's tyrants, and Sister Winn felt a terrible twinge of guilt that she had refused the job herself, thus forcing Hersaaka to be the hated emissary between Bajor and Cardassia, in the person of Gavak-Gavak. The stink of collaboration was already starting to follow Hersaaka about as the odor of animals now adhered to the priestess . . . and it was entirely unjustified, since Hersaaka had no real choice in the matter. Winn prayed for guidance: *Should I have accepted the stain upon myself, and to blazes with the consequences for Bajor when we're finally free of the Cardassian blot?* The Prophets enigmatically remained silent.

Sister Winn had heard of the Orbs, of course; every priest knew of them. *Perhaps someday, I'll look into one and let the light of the Prophets shine fully on me . . . and then I'll know, once and for all.* "For all" was right: if the Prophets found the gazing eye wanting, they were rumored to burn it out, along with the brain of the unworthy owner.

She shook her head, sweeping out the cobwebs of guilt and self-doubt; she couldn't afford those now! Sister Winn had a job, a job that would have been impossible were she as closely monitored as was poor Hersaaka Toos. On her peregrination, she paid especial attention to the movements of the sentries. Like virtually everything else Cardassian, the sentries had ritualized their task to the point of predictability: she watched for only a few minutes and was able to predict where every guard would be at any moment.

In any task that became routine to that extent, there were gaps where nobody was looking in a particular direction at a precise moment; there were several, in fact. Winn knew the pattern would be repeated exactly at the next camp—they *were* Cardassians, after all—subject only to the limitations of the terrain (no farmhouses in that section of Surface 92, for example; Gul Ragat would be in his own pavillion, which was still carefully stowed at the moment).

By the time she finished her circuit of the camp, talking to each Bajoran, as was her primary duty, Resistance or no Resistance, Sister Winn had constructed what she *hoped* was a good escape plan. Because Ragat was so "benevolent" a master by Cardassian standards, escapes from his plantation were quite rare; Bajorans knew the penalty for running away from Gul Ragat's honor farm was either execution, or if the slave escaped that fate, transportation up to *Terok Nor* . . . which might actually be worse: Gul Dukat's cruelty was legendary across all five points of the globe. But the consequence had lulled Gul Ragat's sentries to the point of somnambulation, and she hoped any slop in her plan would fall unnoticed.

When she returned to her own tent, which she shared with two other women, she collapsed suddenly onto her sleeping mat, so exhausted she surprised even herself. As she lay on her back feeling her legs and especially feet throb with every beat of her pulse, she tried to understand her fatigue: she was always tired after a long march, but not this tired! And she had been fine a few moments before, circumnavigating the camp. *It's fear,* she realized at last; *my body is starting to understand just how deadly a game I'm planning.* But there was nothing she could do about that; a priestess could not allow fear of physical death to interfere with a duty of the soul—as she was convinced the fight for Bajor's independence truly was. *I think I know how the holy martyrs felt,* thought Winn bitterly, and she knew the thought was not even blasphemous.

Sister Winn had one more duty that evening, to lead the Bajorans in their prayers over supper. She roused herself at the proper time and led the prayer, then forced her eyes to remain open long enough to eat some food and engage, somewhat incoherently, in a little light banter. She always believed in the necessity of keeping up appearances; appearances were more important than a lot of people admitted: morale was based almost entirely upon the most superficial aspects of one's spiritual leaders, for example. Then as soon as she could reasonably excuse herself, she stumbled back to her tent and fell instantly into a deep sleep, at least two hours before the others.

She woke with a start, heart racing and breath coming quick and heavy, an hour before dawn—a time she rarely saw on a normal day. She could hear only the Bajoran cooks stirring, banging pots, and of course the ever present, clockwork plodding of the Cardassian sentries. She rose too quickly and had to wait for a wash of dizziness to depart as her blood pressure increased. Then, for decency's sake, she wrapped a morning cloak about her already too warm body and walked into the middle of the camp to begin the morning prayers . . . rather earlier than was usual for her.

One of the Cardassian sentries noticed; he was new, and his shift always ended before Sister Winn normally bestirred herself, so he had never seen her move through her rituals. He approached, scowling.

"What d'you think you're doing?"

"I think I'm praying, most gracious sir."

"Why?"

Winn looked up at the boy, no more than twenty, his face stamped with the permanent, ugly sneer of the bully. *I'll bet you tried to join the Obsidian Order and were rejected because of a low IQ,* she thought—then instantly apologized to the Prophets for the uncharity. "Sir, I am praying because I am the sister, the priestess you would say, to all these Bajorans. It is my duty to pray to the Prophets at certain times of the day, morning being one of those times. Overseer Gavak-Gavak Das will vouch for my duties, most benevolent corporal."

She waited politely a moment or two for response, but the boy was still thinking; she returned to her prayers, but he interrupted her once more. "All right, then . . . but get to it! Stop lollygagging, or I'll have you reassigned to hauling luggage." He could do no such thing, of course; Gul Ragat would never allow it. But Winn knew how to handle such bullies as this young corporal: she bowed deeply to the boy and thanked him profusely, promising to speed up the prayers if he so commanded. Then she took exactly as long as she always did, of course; how was he to know? The corporal of the guard stalked off, seemingly pleased that he had pushed around another Bajoran.

Winn started to worry; if the same guard were on

duty tomorrow night when she was to make her escape, he might be especially alert; he was young and only recently transferred to the service of Gul Ragat from . . . from where? Sister Winn remembered with a sinking heart: the corporal was just transferred from the orbital station, *Terok Nor;* he had received his training in the security forces of Gul Dukat! *Yes, this angry child is definitely one to avoid,* she told herself.

The second day's march was so much easier than the first that Sister Winn almost considered commencing an exercise program at the gymnasium at Gul Ragat's; *I must be terribly out of shape!* She had noticed a lot of her clothes getting rather tight in recent months, but she had assumed they were shrinking for some reason.

Healer Daana's footwraps worked wonders. Winn's feet stopped hurting entirely after the first few kilometers, when the circulation really started reaching her toes; Daana had added pads to strategic points in the priestess's shoes as well as wraps to prevent her toes from sliding against each other. By the time Gul Ragat called a halt for the midday meal, Winn felt her excitement growing: *I'm really going to do it!* she nearly said aloud. The horizon seemed so close in the still, chilly air, she thought she might be able to reach out and touch its line.

Surface 92 was so straight and level, it was virtually impossible not to become hypnotized by the steady tramping. The air was too cold for heat mirages, so Winn was denied even that slight solace of illusory motion. But she kept track of their progress by the distance markers. She spent some time mentally calculating where was the closest point to the cabin of Velda Reeks . . . she wasn't sure of the numbers—math was never the priestess's highest subject—but it didn't appear as though they would get quite that far before camping for the night.

Sister Winn *felt* an expletive without even quite vocalizing it to herself, so well-trained was her mind. It meant quite a bit of extra travel through the thigh-deep mud, and more of a chance of misjudging the direction and missing the cabin entirely. It was shielded against Cardassian sensors, after all, so the best she could do was head in approximately the right direction while beaming a tight, low-amplitude message saying who she was, hoping that Velda Reeks found *her.*

IF, she thought, *I can steal a sensor-communicator from the Cardassians, that is.* That made two overt acts before she could escape: break into a skimmer and send it along a false trail and liberate some communications gear. But with her feet feeling so good, Sister Winn was convinced she could do anything!

An idea occurred to her; she increased her pace, passing several ranks of Bajorans and then the gul's Cardassian honor guard. No one moved to stop her; she was well-known among all the gul's intimates.

"My Lord," she said, hurrying to catch up with

Ragat's open-top skimmer limousine, "M'Lord, I must speak to you! It is urgent."

Gul Ragat looked about in surprise; seeing Sister Winn walking beside his car, he automatically tapped the code to open the bird wing door. His bodyguard and Neemak Counselor each grabbed an arm and hoisted the priestess into the car with them.

The guard was just another Cardassian soldier, one of the commissioned officers selected for the honor that day. But Neemak always made Winn's flesh creep: his face was too smooth for a Cardassian, for one point, and he had the faintest suggestion of nose ridges, giving Winn the disturbing impression that he might actually be a cross between Cardassian and Bajoran. His eyes were set too far apart, and his mouth a slight bit too wide; Neemak Counselor had a tendency to look to the left of the person he was addressing, and when he wet his lips, which was frequently, his tongue darted in and out like a reptile.

He didn't dress like a Cardassian, either; he wore a simple red smock with no markings, nothing even to indicate planet of origin. Winn had no idea how good an attorney he was, but he was reputed to "know everyone," which in Cardassian courts probably made him very successful indeed. Neemak stared to the left of Sister Winn while she addressed the gul . . . she knew he was watching her.

"Now, now," said Gul Ragat, making calming

gestures as though she were a frightened child. "What is so important, Sister Winn? Come now, speak up!"

"My Lord, I—" *Well, smart-shoes, what IS so important?* At once, Winn's mind went totally blank. She had thought of something, and it was such a good idea!

"My Lord Gul," said Neemak, his mouth twitching as he stared out the window of the skimmer, "surely your benevolence toward these servants knows no bounds. For I am unaware of any other personage of your exalted rank who would take one of them into his own skimmer. Perhaps we should inquire whether another Bajoran's feet hurt?"

"Yes, ah, yes," mumbled Gul Ragat, tugging at his collar, "I'm sure there's no need to discuss this with anyone . . . is there?" The sudden revelation that the gul was *afraid* of his counselor startled Sister Winn's memory back. "Winn!" snapped Ragat, "what is the urgent news you need to deliver to me? Quick, now! Then you must alight and continue on foot, as is proper."

"My Lord, I have had a most disturbing vision regarding . . . ah, the matter we discussed earlier." She pointedly did not look at Neemak Counselor; Gul Ragat stiffened and licked his lips nervously. *So he didn't even tell his personal secretary!* That clinched the matter; Neemak was connected. Despite the hideous possibility that he was a crossbreed between Cardassian and Bajoran, somebody in the high command—probably either Legate

Migar or Gul Dukat—was using Neemak as eyes and ears upon Gul Ragat . . . and Ragat knew it well.

"What about the matter, Winn?"

"I had infor . . . I mean, I had a vision that things might happen sooner than we thought; as soon as tomorrow morning."

"Morning? You said morning?"

"Yes, My Lord. Late morning. Or so said my—my vision."

"Heh heh heh heh," chuckled the gul, quite unconvincingly, "these superstitious, simple people and their visions!" He leaned close to Neemak and stage-whispered, "She seems to think my palace is going to burn down."

Neemak raised his brows and stared to the left of Gul Ragat. "Indeed, My Lord? Does she not know of the sprinkler system and the fire suppressors?" He turned his head to *almost* look at Winn. "I pity the poor Bajoran *terrorist* who might plot arson against a gul of the Cardassian Empire. So treasonous; so pathetically ineffective."

"Actually," muttered Winn, "my vision was of a lightning strike, Lord Counselor."

Neemak gazed placidly out the window at the bright blue sky; a single, small cumulus cloud drifted lazily across the dome like a seed pod blown from a Prophet's Breath flower. "I recommend," he said, "in my official capacity as my lord's counselor that we consider long and hard before replacing Cardassian meteorology with Bajoran visions of the supernatural, My Lord Gul."

"Yes, quite. Quite so. Yes, quite so." Ragat nodded vigorously. He gestured at the door; without waiting to be ordered, Sister Winn opened it and stepped out, having to jog a bit as the gul's driver sped up slightly . . . *probably on purpose,* thought the priestess in annoyance; again, she quickly apologized to the Prophets for her uncharitable thought. She slowed to a walk and dropped back to her proper place in the processional, wondering whether the seed she had planted would germinate. *I'll know soon enough,* she thought; the sun was starting to sink, and ordinarily, the "kind-hearted" Gul Ragat would call a halt early to give his servants on foot more time to rest. But this day, they continued on into the bone-chilly night.

Four hours later, deep into a black-dark, moonless night, Gavak-Gavak Das finally stopped the column. The grumbling, footsore Bajorans sank in their tracks, massaging calves and wetting their aching, throbbing feet. Beneath the starry canopy of brilliant, pinprick jewels, most yellow white, but a few red giants or blue dwarfs among them, Sister Winn rubbed her own sore feet and tried not to feel guilty for putting her flock to such extra tramping. *Sometimes it is necessary,* she remembered, *to sacrifice a finger to save the hand;* it was a saying attributed to the greatest of all the Prophets . . . but in reality, it could have been said by any doctor, freedom fighter, or tyrant on any planet in the galaxy.

The gul had bought her ruse; he was pushing to reach Riis by early to midmorning, rather than afternoon. In reality, Sister Winn was taking a terrible gamble: arriving earlier, the Cardassians had a greater chance to catch the Resistance cell unaware, if Winn weren't able to warn them in time. But the extra four hours put the night's camp *much* closer to the sensor-shielded shack of Velda Reeks, and actually gave Winn a fighting chance of finding the woman and alerting her, so she could communicate with the cell and call off the strike on the spaceport.

It felt like a fifty-fifty proposition to Sister Winn, but it was the best she could do. All that remained were three impossible feats: liberating a communicator from the Cardassians, reprogramming one of the guard's skimmers, and escaping across four kilometers of foot-sucking mud to find an invisible cabin in a trackless wasteland.

Sister Winn felt a great peace settle upon her; *it's all in the hands of the Prophets now,* she thought . . . *but my faith would certainly be strengthened by a personal cloaking device.*

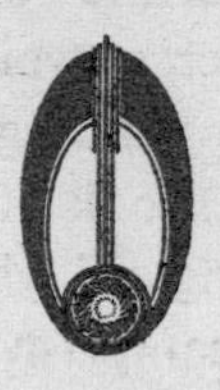

CHAPTER 8

SISTER WINN's greatest fear, she was ashamed to admit to anyone but Those she served, was that she would fall asleep for real and sleep right through her own escape. She had to feign sleep—closed eyes, rhythmic breath, inert body, sneaking not even a scratch of the side of her nose or wiping the thin trail of drool that trickled down her chin.

Her roommates were several girls from the village and one, Mali, from the palace itself; and Winn suspected that at least one of the girls was a Cardassian informant: her cell leader, whose name she never heard, told her it was "SOP"—standard operating procedure—for the Cardassians to constantly monitor all Bajoran leaders . . . even down to the village mayor level. Surely a full, ordained sister priestess, one of the youngest ever invested, would qualify for such surveillance!

She kept awake by running through all seventy-seven prayers of the Book of Amakira, a test she had passed as a young girl while studying for holy orders; each prayer comprised sixteen syllables, so it took quite some time to pass through the entire book, especially while fully comprehending the *meaning* of each verse: Sister Winn had great need for the heart-comforting revelations of Amakira. When she finished, the camp was silent, save for the omnipresent tramp of the guards; *same rhythm as last night, thank the Prophets.*

Winn had made sure she took the sleeping mat closest to the tent flap. She rose so excruciatingly slowly and quietly, she was actually startled when her elbow joint cracked. Winn rolled to her knees, then pressed back to the balls of her feet. Technically, it was forbidden for a Bajoran to leave his tent during the night; but Gul Ragat, though terribly young—no more than twenty-one years old!—was aware that many older folk had only half-a-night bladders, and he never strictly enforced the rule, so long as the trek was straight to the relief station and straight back to the tent. If challenged, or even if spotted, Winn was prepared to abort her plans and head straight for the privy.

She gingerly plucked her shoes from beneath the pile of other girls' footgear and ghosted through the tent flap before putting them on. Outside, she stepped into the shadow of the tent and surveyed the scene.

She had picked a good night for an escape. The moon was new, and they were far enough along Surface 92 that no city lights illuminated the clear, star-spattered sky. The road itself occupied the central strip of the causeway; there was a parade ground or picnic area (Winn wasn't sure why the Cardassians had built it) extending like an apron on either side of the actual road, widening every so often, and it was on the eastern side of the apron that Gul Ragat's entourage was encamped. The parade ground was paved with a plastic-polymer that was somewhat springy to the foot, and it was colored green . . . a creepy, Cardassian imitation of a grassy sward, Winn supposed. In any event, her soft shoes made no noise as she slid from one end of the tent to the other, peeking around the edges at the guards.

Her heart pounded so hard, her chest actually hurt. She stared hungrily at the parked skimmer cycles of the guards; *probably have a communications wand on one of the skimmers,* she told herself . . . though it was really just a guess. If the Prophets were with her, it was an educated one.

Timing her movements to the disappearance of all three guards behind various tents, Winn hunched over and ran as quickly as she could manage to the cycles. She was already huffing and blowing by the time she covered the short distance, wishing she had paid more attention to such fleshy matters as her weight and physical conditioning. *There's such a thing as being too spiritual, I guess,* she decided.

The cycles loomed much larger up close than they had when they hummed past her on the march; Cardassians tended to be larger than Bajorans—or taller, anyway—and Sister Winn was somewhat on the short side even for her sex and species. She stole in between the first two: *If I'm caught now,* she realized, *there is no possible way to explain . . . nobody's going to believe I got lost on the way to the privy!* The machines hulked black and menacing in the moonless dark, but the metal was actually shiny enough that if she raised her head and looked at the top of the stabilizer wings, she saw the constellations dimly reflected. She smelled ozone as the fuel cells recharged the batteries in preparation for another day of travel.

She heard the tramp of boots; a sentry approached along his normal route. Winn couldn't move; it would only attract his attention. She wasn't fully in shadow, but she stilled her body and held her breath.

The sentry strode into view; he was close enough that she could have hit him with a stone. If he turned his head just slightly to the right, he couldn't help seeing her!

Winn looked down, superstitiously worrying about "catching his eye" by staring at him herself. She envisioned herself shrinking inside herself, like a snake swallowing its own tail until there was nothing left but a faint puff of displaced air.

The measured crunching of boot steps continued unwavering past the priestess and into the night. The sentry had passed her by unnoticed. She had several minutes before he returned, and Sister Winn had every intention of taking full advantage.

She had seen the Cardassians using their communication wands, and it was an article of faith for the priestess that anything a Cardassian could learn to operate would be child's play for a Bajoran. But would they leave them on the cycles or take them inside their own tents?

She found no wand on the first two cycles, though she was somewhat hampered in her search by not being able to rise up and lean over to look at the other side of the first skimmer; taking a deep breath and gritting her teeth, as if she were diving into the ocean, she slipped around cycle number two and explored its left side and the right side of cycle three.

At last, the priestess struck a vein of pure ore: she found not one but two communication wands stuck into the left saddlebag of cycle number seven. But then she heard the tramp of the sentry, now coming in the opposite direction. Again, she didn't move, didn't breathe, and visualized herself shrinking to a dust mote, smaller and smaller to the vanishing point. Evidently, the sentry was either asleep on his feet or else he simply had no reason to look at the parked skimmer cycles; once again, he walked past her, almost close enough for Winn to reach out and untie his bootlaces (were he wearing any).

When her heart returned to only a moderately fast beat, she slipped one of the com-wands into her voluminous sleeve pocket. Then, licking her dry lips, she commenced the second part of her adventure.

The program controls on the cycles were easy to comprehend . . . assuming one understood Cardassian. Winn had made a point of it when she studied for her holy orders; all official communications to the Cardassian High Command for anything or about anything had to be written in High Cardassian—and the only alternative to learning the language herself was to hire someone to translate every time she had some important request to make, which was not only expensive but dangerous, considering her "night job." The seventh cycle was locked, but the eighth still had a key card in the active slot—a common enough lapse of security for which one of the Cardassian soldiers was going to pay dearly!

She slid the card out and in again, and the console cover slid open with a noise that was probably tiny, but which sounded to the priestess's ears like a dozen pots and pans rattling down a chimney. She scanned the instructions on the inside of the cover, then programmed the cycle on a course that would take it due east for a while, then veer off course in several erratic directions, climbing and diving, finally (if all went well) burying itself in the mud at peak velocity hundreds of kilometers from Surface 92 . . . followed, she hoped, by a parade of frantic Cardassians, desperate to stop the Amazing Escaping Priestess.

In fact, the A.E.P. would be heading on foot the opposite direction, equally desperately trying to locate the Amazing Invisible Cabin of Velda Reeks. Winn had only to set the timer, then cut across the road without being run over by the occasional truck or troop transport, and jump off the western edge without killing herself in the fall. *Simplicity itself,* she thought, clenching her teeth to keep them from chattering with fear.

She calculated the distance across the eastern apron, the road—assuming she didn't become roadkill—and the opposite apron, then over the side to the mud, and came up with a ludicrous figure that sounded more like the time required by the Bajoran sprint champion. She doubled the time, then on second thought tripled it, and programmed it into the cycle's control panel. She was about to activate the timer when she realized she would run smack into the sentries if she didn't time the run exactly right.

Winn waited, following the sentries' position by the sound of their boot heels on the springy surface of the parade ground . . . she wouldn't have heard them at all except for the metal heel-and-toe protectors—Cardassian soldiers disdained the idea of stealth, though the priestess was fairly sure the spies of the Obsidian Order didn't wear steel-shod boots. When she judged they had reached about halfway between the nearest point (where she would have to run directly past them) and the farthest point (where they turned around and would be looking right at her as she fled), she punched the button and took off.

Halfway to the edge of the apron, Winn realized she had *severely* underestimated the time it would take for her to run that distance! She felt her heart pound and she was gasping for air, so she slowed to a trot, too frightened even to appeal to the Prophets for assistance. When she passed the last row of tents and could see the backs of the two sentries receding, she panicked; spurred by terror, she stepped up the pace to a sprint again . . . but after only a dozen steps, she stumbled and fell to her face.

The soft, springy surface prevented her from scraping herself or making much sound, but she landed on her belly and knocked the wind from her lungs. She tried to stagger to her feet, while her bruised diaphragm fluttered, unable to expand to suck in a lungful of air. She felt dizzy, so she remained on hands and knees and crawled toward the center road section of Surface 92.

Just as she reached it, she heard a roar; looking to her left, she saw the lights of an onrushing truck, skimming a mere hand's breadth above the road surface; it was almost as wide as the road itself. Winn mentally cursed her luck—if the truck were going south instead of north, it would have been traveling high enough to clear the northbound trucks, and the priestess could have run directly beneath it! Instead, she was delayed precious seconds while the truck lumbered past at half the speed of a passenger skimmer. Ironically, it had doubtless slowed down because the sensors detected the encampment, and the polite driver (who was probably Bajoran) didn't want to wake them up with loud engine noise.

Winn waited, lying on her belly; though the delay surely meant the skimmer cycle would take off before she was off the opposite side, it did give her a chance to catch her breath. With the help of the Prophets, the sentries might not even notice the cycle launching. Sister Winn prayed earnestly for just such a stroke of good fortune.

Evidently, the Prophets were unmoved by her prayers. Just as the truck cleared her path, Winn heard an awful racket back at the camp: the cycle was taking off just as she programmed, with one slight addition: it had automatically activated its flashing lights and warning siren. With a sinking heart, she realized she must have picked, by sheer bad luck, the lead cycle of the procession.

Winn stared back in horror as the riderless cycle rose into the air, screaming bloody, blue murder like a hysterical child and lighting up the entire camp with its red-and-green strobe lights. Within seconds, every Cardassian soldier was stumbling out of his tent more or less dressed, each with a weapon in hand; the Bajorans rushed out, too, adding to the chaos. Everyone stared at the ghostly apparition . . . and that meant that no one would mistakenly believe Sister Winn had stolen the skimmer when she turned up missing.

She hesitated at the edge of the road, not knowing what to do. Then, hoping that she wouldn't be missed for quite some time in the hullabaloo, she resumed course for the opposite side of Surface 92, this time walking quickly and keeping her heart rate down.

She crossed the road and the western apron and stared over the opposite side; it was a drop of ten meters, a hard fall but not likely to permanently damage her, if she landed well. She felt no fear; she had totally drained whatever glandular secretion caused it. She turned about and lowered herself over the side, dangling by her hands.

It was a posture she couldn't hold for more than a few seconds; she had only time enough to take one last look back at the cavorting, screaming mob. It was an unfortunate whim: just as she looked, one of the sentries, her old friend, the young, bullying corporal, turned on a whim of his own toward the priestess. Their eyes locked for a moment; before he could react, the strength gave out in Winn's hands, and she dropped heavily into the mud. Her only thought as she fell was, *Oh dear, I really have made a mess of the whole thing.*

She landed on her back in the mud and again

knocked the wind from her sails. She remained perfectly still, waiting for the dizziness to stop and staring at the lip of the road above her, wondering whether she would be able to move before the demoted corporal peered over the edge and saw her. She was so shaken, the possibility of being seen again didn't rouse her to any greater effort.

What shook her awake at last was the cry of a child—a *child!* Instinct took over, both as a woman and as a representative of the Prophets, and the priestess struggled up to her feet. She walked under the road, the mud sucking at her feet with every step, threatening to pull her under like tar; the child could be no more than a few years old, judging by the sound . . . but Winn could tell nothing more about it.

She looked but saw nothing; there was one large support pillar big enough to hide a small person, and Winn headed for it. The child was crouching behind, the only place it could be. Mud was caked so heavily on its face that Winn couldn't even tell whether it was a boy or girl . . . not that it would have been easy in any event, since the child (like Gul Ragat's counselor) was another abomination: half Cardassian, half Bajoran.

For some reason, however, this mixture aroused only pity in the priestess's soul, rather than the revulsion she usually experienced. *Because it's only a child,* she thought to herself, but it was more, and she knew it. Unlike Neemak Counselor, this child's face showed only fear and shame, not the cynical cruelty stamped on the face of the other cross-breeds she had seen . . . *a cruelty incubated by the way such mongrels were treated—by both sides,* thought Winn with a very large thrust of guilt.

"It's all right, honey, I've got you," she said soothingly. The child only cried the harder; slightly cleaner channels ran down its cheeks where streams of tears had partially washed away the mud. "You're going to be all right, child; I promise." Winn smiled. "I know I don't look it, but under all this mud, I'm a sister, a voice of the Prophets. I'm not going to hurt you."

"Going to turn me over," said the child . . . and Sister Winn decided it was probably a girl.

"To whom, little one?"

The girl looked away. Above, Winn heard shouts and the engines of several skimmers; the corporal had obviously reported what he saw to the captain of the guard, and the Cardassians were coming over the edge of the road to hunt for her.

"I won't lie to you, child. The Cardassians are about to come down here hunting for me, and they're going to use sensors, and they're going to find you, too. There's nothing either one of us can do about that."

"Why're they after you?" asked the little girl, eyes wide; she sniffled, but she seemed to have forgotten about crying. She could be no more than four years old.

Winn shrugged, deciding on the truth—as much as the girl could handle. *The Prophets obviously brought us together; there must still be a task for me ahead.* "I ran away, child. I'm a slave. I wanted to leave, and now they're going to bring me back."

The little girl smiled sadly. "I guess they're going to send me back to father. But you're a nice lady."

"Thank you."

The girl looked at Winn; her eyes held the priestess in a gaze so intelligent, so intense, that Winn suddenly realized the Prophets themselves were about to speak through the child's lips. She had heard of such things but never seen it directly. All sound seemed to cease; she could hear nothing but the words from the little girl: "Tell them you heard me crying and jumped down here to help me, Mother Mud. Then you won't get in trouble. My father is very important."

"Who is your father?"

"He lives in the sky," she said, pointing upward. "He's very important, and they'll be happy you found me." Her face took on a look of urgency. "Tell them! Promise me you'll tell them you jumped down to help me!"

Sister Winn bowed her head. "I promise, child." A moment later, the fist skimmer roared up to her, followed by three others. One was ridden by Gavak-Gavak Das himself, and Winn braced for a lashing with the electrowhip the overseer always carried.

"I heard the cries of this child," said the priestess. "I jumped off the road and followed the cries to this little girl."

"She found me," added the girl. "I want to go home." Winn knew that both of them were liars, but perhaps it was in a good cause.

Gavak-Gavak paused astride his cycle, his mouth open and his hand already having drawn the painful whip. Struck by sudden concern, he replaced the electrowhip and drew a scanner instead. Playing it across the girl, he gasped and spoke urgently but softly into his communications wand; Winn couldn't hear a word he said.

Then the overseer grinned, and Winn recognized the expression: pure, unadulterated greed. *There must be a reward out for the little girl,* thought the priestess sadly.

"Excellent work, Sister Winn!" said Gavak-Gavak unexpectedly. "I'll see that you're commended to the gul for this!"

"You'll tell Gul Ragat what happened?"

"Ragat?" The overseer looked startled. "Oh! Yes, that's what I meant . . . I'll see that you're commended to Gul Ragat for your diligence in finding—ah, this little girl here. I'm sure her master is terribly anxious to get her back, ah, whoever he is."

Nobody ever accused Sister Winn of mental sluggishness. She noticed the quick change of subject; Gavak-Gavak had originally meant another gul, but he preferred she think he was talking about her own. And she noticed another strange anomaly: Gavak-Gavak referred to the girl's *master,* but the girl said that her *father* was very important. *We are not given to understand all the ways of the Prophets,* thought the priestess; *we are bound only to obey them.* She said nothing else, only climbed aboard the back of one of the other skimmers to be carried back to servitude, back to the road to Riis.

CHAPTER 9

THE BLUFF from which O'Brien and the away team had looked out across the Desert of Death (as the chief had cheerfully named it) sloped backward a dozen kilometers to a grassy sward; the team had to backtrack several hours before Odo, flying above as a hawk, caught sight of a herd of the creatures . . . split-heads, Chief O'Brien dubbed them. The constable circled overhead while the rest of the team caught up; Odo landed, and the away team remained behind an outcropping of blue black rocks to observe the nine split-heads.

Two different families, guessed the chief; that is, if they followed the pattern of Earth horses, or the other horselike creatures O'Brien had read about. There were two larger split-heads with short, tubelike tails, and each was surrounded by three smaller monsters with no tails. One of the groups included what looked like a foal: tiny, with overly long, skinny legs that followed around one of the smaller split-heads. Captain Sisko began speaking of the larger as male and the smaller as female, and the nomenclature stuck, though they had no real idea about the beasties' gender traits.

Their coats ranged from sky blue to teal, and they could bristle their spiney fur, possibly for cooling or defense or both. O'Brien hadn't seen any of them jump, but he suspected they could deliver a vicious kick if you got behind one; he had once been kicked in a sensitive spot by an ordinarily placid mare back home, and he still squirmed when he remembered the experience. "Sir, are you sure this rope will hold those things?" he asked nervously.

"Chief, you know the tensile strength of the polyfiber better than I! It could hoist a runabout without breaking." Captain Sisko seemed quite irritated . . . possibly because the chief had been hedging and hesitating for several minutes. The truth was, even the sight of the horrible beasties terrified him: Quark was right; the split down the center of their skulls really did make them look two-headed. And the six bowlegs that seemed to be as common on the planet as four (the Natives were four limbed, of course) still made the chief squirm; it looked a little too *insectoid* for his taste.

"All right," said the chief, straining to keep his

voice steady and his teeth from chattering, "let's do it. Commander?"

Worf stared at the herd. "I recommend we try for the male with the dark hindquarters; it is smaller than the other."

"Sure, whichever; go ahead, sir."

They had necessarily opted against using phasers because of the danger of being spotted by Cardassians in orbit. O'Brien fidgeted, fingering the lasso, while the Klingon waited until the target wandered away from the other split-heads; then Worf activated the antigrav and levitated the great beast into the air.

Miles O'Brien stood and jogged into the clearing, keeping an eye on the other creatures. He was just about to fling the loop of rope, when he stopped dead: he heard voices, and they seemed to come from the split-heads surrounding him:

"Arrk fly!"

"Fly! Fly in the air!"

"Look at Arrk! He flies in the air!"

With horror creeping along his skin like a fungus, Chief O'Brien realized that the universal translator was automatically translating what the animals were saying . . . and that meant *they were talking*. Arrk himself, from his position about three or four meters in the air, began screaming; the universal translator left most of it inarticulate, but did translate "help" and "get Arrk down."

O'Brien backed slowly away from the herd, which totally ignored his presence, so focused were they on their compatriot's sudden levity. The chief finally stumbled backwards over a rock, falling onto his rear where the rest of the away team waited.

"Well?" demanded Worf; "what is the problem?"

Sisko was even more irritated. "Chief, you had better have a *damned* good explanation for this!"

O'Brien turned to the captain. "They're intelligent! They were talking . . . words, not just growling or barking or somesuch!"

Sisko tightened his lips and stroked his beard; everybody else stared at O'Brien as if he were addlepated. "Of all the idiotic excuses!" snapped Quark; "don't be afraid of them . . . just get out there and rope a few!" Nevertheless, the chief noted that Quark made no offer to do the job himself.

"I'm telling you, those things are *talking!* They're out there screaming about how 'Arrk' is flying around in the sky. If you don't believe me," he added huffily, "just wander closer and you'll hear them yourself."

Sisko frowned. "This changes everything, Worf. Put the creature down."

With a sigh of complete exasperation, Worf lowered Arrk to the ground. The bull split-head ran around in circles for a few minutes, followed by the others; then they all seemed to calm down and return to grazing . . . seeming to have forgotten the incident. *If they are sentient,* thought O'Brien, *it's only just barely.*

"Wait here," said the captain; O'Brien was only too happy to oblige: the only thing worse than a two-headed, six-legged horse was one that talked. Sisko stepped forward, gesturing to Worf to follow. The pair crept closer to the herd; when they got within twenty meters, the split-heads looked up one by one. Then they returned to their grazing, paying no attention to the two Federation interlopers.

The captain and Worf returned, the former pensive and the latter frowning. "Chief, I owe you an apology," said Captain Sisko. "I should have believed you, no matter how crazy it sounded." Worf merely grunted, but O'Brien took it as the closest to an apology he was likely to get from his Klingon colleague.

"What did they say, sirs?"

Worf took up the tale. "When we approached, they queried each other whether we were four-legged or six-legged. After some discussion, they settled that we were four-legged; after that, they ignored us completely."

"I would guess," chimed in Odo, "that all their natural predators have six legs, as they themselves do."

"So," mused Quark, "not only can they talk—they can count . . ." His eyes rolled up, and O'Brien imagined he could see stacks of gold-pressed latinum whirling around, like the spin of a

Dabo wheel. "I wonder," continued the Ferengi, "whether any of these split-heads has any interest in a small exhibition we might—"

"Quark!" snarled the constable. "We have more important considerations at hand, *if* you don't mind!"

"Exactly," said the captain, sitting on a rock in plain view of the herd. "I'm afraid these creatures pass the threshhold of sentience . . . we cannot simply yoke them to a wagon and force them to carry us across the desert."

"So now what?" asked the chief. "Correct me if I'm wrong, but don't we only have three or four days of rations left? If we don't get to a Cardassian outpost by then, we can kiss both the mission and our own, lovely selves goodbye." It was a simple conclusion: as disgusting as it was, Cardassian food was the only thing on Sierra-Bravo 112-II that any of them could eat and remain alive.

"Time," said Captain Sisko with a twinkle and a half smile, "to open negotiations."

"Negotiations?" demanded both the chief and Commander Worf in astonishment.

"And to send in our chief negotiator," concluded the captain. "Ambassador Quark, front and center!"

"Ambassador Quark?" sputtered Constable Odo, with even greater astonishment.

Sisko clapped the Ferengi on his shoulder. "You wanted to come along on this expedition," he said; "it's time you earned your keep: start bargaining, and don't come back without an agreement to convey us to that outpost!"

Quark said nothing. His mouth opened as he stared at the monstrous creatures. *Better thee than me,* thought Chief O'Brien with a smile.

The Ferengi had never felt tinier and more helpless as he crept toward the enormous, two-headed monsters. Among Ferengi, Quark was actually rather on the tall side, and even among the giants on *Deep Space Nine,* under whatever name they chose to operate it, past or future, he always knew he was in control: the man at the helm of his own destiny *never* feels small!

But these creatures, Quark was convinced, were too stupid to recognize their own self-interest . . . and they could very well trample him to death before he could even finish making his opening bid. Quark looked back at the sheltering rocks; the other members of the away team were gesturing him forward impatiently. *Sure! Of course . . . THEY'RE not the ones facing death by hoof-stomping!*

He felt a faint movement from behind him and whipped his head back so quickly, his neckbones cracked, and he felt a sharp pain. The split-heads, as Chief O'Brien so quaintly called them, were staring directly at Quark.

Centimeter by centimeter, the Ferengi snuck forward across the blue gray grass, feeling his legs weakening with every quasi step. He raised his hand, only belatedly worrying that the monsters might consider that an attack. So far, they hadn't said anything . . . if indeed they really did talk; he hadn't quite ruled out the possibility that the whole thing was an elaborate and pointless practical joke played upon him by the Federation goons.

"How—how—how do you d-do?" The horrible-looking monsters stared uncomprehendingly at him. "I am Quark," he added, "I . . . come in peace." No response. "Shall we, ah, open negotiations?"

Suddenly feeling utterly stupid, Quark realized he was, in essence, talking to a herd of barnyard animals. His face turned bright pink, and he began to yell. "Say something, damn it! I'm feeling like an idiot here!"

One of the large split-heads, a male, Quark supposed, turned to the other. "It is Quark the Idiot!"

"Yes, yes," bleated the other male; "Quark the Idiot! What is an Idiot?"

The females took up the refrain, repeating "Idiot! Idiot!" over and over. They seemed positively fascinated by the concept . . . if the universal translator were doing its job, it might be the first time the thought had ever occurred to them.

"A small-head," suggested the first male, who seemed to be the leader. "That's what an Idiot is."

"Yes, yes! An Idiot is a small-head! Look, it's head is small. Look how small its head is! And look, look . . . *no horns!*"

The animals proceeded to make a series of *gronk*like noises that Quark rather stuffily took to be untranslated laughter.

"Does it have four legs or does it have six legs?" asked the junior male.

"I will count the legs," responded the alpha. "One leg, two legs, three legs, four legs. It's a four-leg! A four-legged, small-headed Idiot called Quark."

"Four legs," sighed the beta male that O'Brien claimed they had called Arrk; once he realized Quark had only four limbs, Arrk immediately lost interest. The steel-blue grass beckoned the rest of the split-heads; the alpha watched the Ferengi for a few moments, then joined the rest of the herd in grazing. One of the presumed females—who had a smaller head than the other monsters—began to trot round and round the herd, chanting, "Small-head! Idiot! Small-head! Idiot!" The others ignored her.

"Oh, this is going just perfectly," muttered Quark to himself. His annoyance battled against fear and won; he walked a little closer, but the split-heads still ignored him. "Listen!" commanded the Ferengi.

One by one, the monsters stopped grazing and raised their heads to look down their split noses at Quark. "We want a deal," he enunciated clearly, wondering whether the word would even translate. Evidently not; the creatures all looked to the alpha, who stared at Quark in puzzlement.

"We want to go . . . past the sand," said the Ferengi, pointing upslope.

"It wants sand," said the alpha male to Arrk.

"It eats sand," suggested the latter.

The alpha said, "Yes, yes! It eats sand so its head is small! It should eat grass."

"I *don't* eat sand!" shouted Quark, stamping his foot. *That,* he realized, was a bad move; the alpha lowered its head and snarled.

"Challenging, challenging, challenging!" it said. "Small-head is challenging Ruut!"

Uh-oh . . . Staring up at the huge, many-toothed, horned monster that looked as if it could tear his (tiny) head off in a single bite or crush his rib cage with a kick, Quark's Ferengi instincts took over: he dropped immediately into an approved cringe, almost a grovel, as if he stood naked before the Grand Nagus himself with a highly negative balance sheet. Quark did it quicker than conscious thought, but if he had had time to plan, it was exactly what he would have done anyway.

The posture worked; the alpha—Ruut—instantly relaxed, muttering, "Small-head loses, Ruut wins."

The female began to trot again, repeating her chant of "Small-head! Idiot!"

"Small-head wants a favor from Ruut," said Quark, wrinkling his nose at the name he seemed to have acquired.

"What does small-head want?" asked Ruut, surprised. Evidently, a favor was not unheard of—

probably has to do with not killing an annoying female, thought Quark. But it seemed uncommon.

"Small-head and, uh, small-head's herd want to get to the grass on the other side of the sand."

"The grass is better?" asked Arrk; Ruut didn't seem put out by the interruption.

"Well . . . it's bluer," improvised Quark.

"The grass is bluer!" shouted Ruut.

"Where? Where?" bleated the females; Arrk took up the chant, evidently not quite following the conversation as well as the alpha.

"In the meadow on the other side of the big sand!" exclaimed Ruut. "Across the sand, bluer, tastier grass! Small-head knows!"

"But small-head is an Idiot," objected Arrk.

Ruut thought a moment, then extended his face until his mouth was pressed practically against Quark's nose. The Ferengi was too terrified to move or even speak; he smelled a sweet odor with a faint whiff of what he could swear was latinum . . . and the trace braced him. "How does small-head know the blueness of the grass?" asked Ruut.

"A wise question," said Quark, his voice shaking. "I—uh—I was—told about it," he finished, lamely.

"Who told small-head about the grass?" persisted the ever suspicious Ruut.

A brilliant idea whispered into the Ferengi's lobes. "I was told," he said, "by a *BIG*-head! A great, big head . . . head the size of Ruut's whole body!"

This information was suitably relayed by Ruut to the rest of the herd, who needed some explanation before they all got it. The trotting female changed her chant to "Small-head! Big-head! Small-head! Big-head!" and Quark wasn't quite sure she understood the fine point he had made. But the others seemed satisfied.

"But small-head has a problem," said the Ferengi. He waited, having learnt that one couldn't rush the monsters' sluggish brains.

"Small-head wants to go to the grass on the other side of the Big Sands," said Ruut.

"But small-head is too slow," said Quark, "and Ruut's herd is much faster. Small-head's herd wants to sit on Ruut's herd while Ruut's herd runs across the Big Sands." The complexity of the suggestion took many minutes to negotiate, but Quark was starting to catch the rhythm. Experimentally, Ruut allowed Quark to sit on Arrk's back while the split-head walked, then trotted, then ran around the meadow. Quark clutched the spiny fur on the monster's back, closed his eyes, and prayed to the Final Accountant not to kill the deal by letting Quark fall off and be trampled to death. The creature had a peculiar, rolling gait not unlike an Earth *camel* that Quark was once obliged to ride in a customer's holosuite program, but when it got up to speed, the wind whistled past the Ferengi's lobes . . . the split-heads were *fast* when they wanted.

Ruut and Arrk had a long conversation afterward, the slow pace of which frustrated the Ferengi no end; he consoled himself by thinking, *The riskier the road, the greater the profit,* and other gems from the Rules of Acquisition. At last, Arrk convinced Ruut that he had barely felt the "small-head" on his back, and there was no reason not to carry the small-head's herd across the Big Sands.

Shaking with exhaustion and the remnants of fear, Quark concluded the deal. As he structured it in his mind, in exchange for the knowledge that there was much bluer grass across the desert, Ruut and his herd would carry Quark and *his* herd across said desert as quickly as possible. The only snag, of course, was that the grass might *not* be bluer on the other side; Quark shrugged . . . the thought that a customer might not be satisfied with his end of the bargain concerned a Ferengi not at all (in fact, it was Rule of Acquisition Number Nineteen). Quark would let Captain Sisko deal with possible future customer complaints.

Ruut figured they would start immediately—did he even have the concept of time or waiting?—and Quark didn't want to tip the precarious deal; he assumed the split-heads' attention span was limited, and he was afraid that any delay would cause Ruut to forget everything. Quark frantically waved Sisko, O'Brien, Worf, and Odo to approach.

A new problem erupted: Ruut and Arrk balked at allowing the away team to ride the females. Small-head's herd huddled to solve the last-minute dilemma.

Odo sighed. "I suppose I could change into one of these creatures myself," he suggested. "That eliminates one of us needing a ride."

"Two of us," corrected Captain Sisko. "I hate to say it, Constable, but you'll have to carry one of us on your back."

Odo shrugged. "I can do that . . . so long as it isn't *him!*" He glared at Quark.

"Captain! I object to the continual calumnies and unfriendly insinuations cast by Odo against me!" He folded his arms and turned half away, making sure everyone saw how his feelings were wounded. "And after all I've done for this team, too."

"You've 'done' at least four serious felonies on this expedition so far," snarled Odo, "and the mission has barely begun! I'm keeping an arrest report," concluded the constable, ominously pushing his malleable face close to Quark's.

"Gentlemen, settle it later," said Sisko. "Quark, you'll double up with me on one of the males, while Worf, who weighs as much as the two of us combined, will ride the other male. That leaves O'Brien for Odo, and you two will be our guides: the chief with his tricorder, the constable by changing into a bird as necessary and finding the fastest route across the desert. Any questions?"

Worf looked at Ruut, the alpha, and Quark would have sworn he saw nervousness in the Klingon's mouth; of course, the Ferengi said nothing—Klingons were generally not appreciative for having such facts pointed out to them. "I have no questions, Captain," said Worf in a tougher-than-usual voice. *Good,* thought Quark, *at least I'm not the only one who's scared to death!* O'Brien made no attempt to hide his relief at drawing Odo instead of Ruut or Arrk, but the captain was as enigmatic as usual.

Quark was trembling as he climbed back aboard Arrk, and the addition of Captain Sisko seated behind him did not sweeten the deal: the Ferengi suspected it made the whole arrangement even more top-heavy and subject to collapse than when Quark alone had ridden the monster!

Worf mounted Ruut. The constable wandered away behind a tree, then returned as a split-head; neither Ruut nor any of his herd seemed to care much or wonder at the transformation. O'Brien climbed aboard Odo, and the caravan set out. They traveled not up the bluff, of course, since that would have required leaping off a hundred-meter cliff, but around it to the left; Ruut seemed to know the way to the Big Sands.

By the time the double herd reached a downward slope, where the grass became sparser and interspersed with sand and the occasional boulder, they were fairly flying; Quark forgot everything except hanging on for dear life and dearer profit. He stopped screaming when his voice became so hoarse, even his sensitive lobes couldn't hear it.

The mob of monsters hit the desert sands and kept going, their monstrous, splay hooves barely sinking into the dunes. They ran tirelessly for hours, then stopped so abruptly, they almost unseated their riders. Odo ran on a few paces before realizing Ruut had called a rest stop.

After a drink at a stream and a short rest, the caravan continued its break-your-neck pace across the sand dunes . . . and after many more hours, Quark discovered that when a Ferengi is exhausted enough, he can doze off *anywhere.*

CHAPTER 10

LIEUTENANT COMMANDER Jadzia Dax was very, very, *very* tired of walking, but they still had a few more kilometers to go until they reached the spot where Bashir had detected a crossing of ion trails from Cardassian skimmers of various sizes. *A crossing means a depot,* Dax told herself . . . the wild promise being the only way she could will her exhausted feet to keep moving. Julian, of course, seemed as fresh as a teenaged boy on a prom date.

The road they followed was obviously not built by the Cardassians; it wound around hills where the Cardassians would simply have burnt right through them with excavating tools. In places, the road was little more than a footpath, zigzagging steeply up a hill and dropping equally suddenly down the far slope. The up and down burned through Dax's energy far more than a simple, level path would have; she couldn't help a sidelong glance or two at the doctor. Oddly, the good doctor seemed much less fatigued than she would have expected from the hike.

They were currently on a section of the road where the trail had virtually disappeared, visible only as a slightly trampled line of steel blue among the rest of the knee-high grass; but at least it was still heading roughly the right direction. Gnarled trees surrounded them, black in the gathering dusk; under the bright, noon sun, they had appeared more vermillion. The long shadows reached toward Dax and Bashir from behind, like clutching fingers; the commander shivered, wishing she hadn't thought of the image: they still had little idea what dangerous fauna (or even flora!) existed on Sierra-Bravo 112-II.

A large set of hills blocked their path, and Dax sighed audibly. They rested before beginning the climb. Bashir insisted, claiming he was "fatigued," but he didn't look it. Then she led the way, setting her sights grimly on the summit and trudging up the twenty-degree slope.

As she neared the top, she slowed; they were close enough that if there were no intervening hills, they might be able to see the intersection . . . the "depot." At the peak of the trail, she found a grove of trees; slipping within them, she worked her way forward, Bashir at her elbow, until she looked out across a plain crossed with natural orchards and watered by a sluggish, winding river.

Most of the valley was already in shadows from the hill Dax and Bashir stood upon. Two strings of bright, artificial lights crossed near the center, lighting the darkness, and a contingent of four Cardassians stood guard at the crossroads: they had found their depot.

"Any skimmers?" asked the doctor, trying to peer past Dax's head.

"I see a couple, one single-seater and a large car, but there's a couple pairs of goons guarding them." *Damn,* she thought, *I'd give a lot for a good, old-fashioned spyglass!*

On a hunch, Dax pulled up her tricorder and performed a passive scan for broadcast power sources of the frequency used by the Natives. "Yep, I suspected as much," she announced. "They cut the power from the nearest two transmitters . . . none of the native technology will work anywhere within a dozen kilometers or more."

"So they think they're totally secure," said Bashir, seeing the point at once.

Dax looked back at him. "Would you say Cardassians are apt to be overconfident under any circumstances?"

"I'd say," said the doctor with a smile, "that the guards are probably asleep on their feet from boredom."

"How good a shot are you with your phaser, Julian?"

"Using a sweep, I can pick off a Cardassian or a Drek'la at about two hundred meters, I would expect."

"Two hundred? That's a little ambitious. Let's get a little closer than that," she decided. "We'll take them at a hundred. One clean sweep apiece, phasers on stun, nobody left standing."

Dax considered for a moment. "But we have to make sure they don't wake up any time soon."

That is, unless we leave our fingerprints somewhere—like here. Jadzia pondered for a moment; what would the Cardassian commander believe? "Maybe we can make it look like they got drunk and deserted? What have you got in that little black bag of yours that might do the trick?"

Julian thought for a moment. "I could inject them with a stasis sedative that will keep them out for about eight hours."

"What will they remember?"

"Nothing; microamnesia will almost certainly wipe out any memory they have of events for the last three or four hours before they're injected."

"That'll be perfect. If we find any Cardassian ale in the depot storehouse, we'll pour it all over them; if we're lucky, they won't bother with a medical scan. Then we'll stick them in the big skimmer and program it to head out over the hills, landing about three hundred klicks away." Dax grinned at the thought. "Let's see them try to explain *that* to the CO!"

The pair of double shots from a hundred meters

required only coordination between Jadzia and Julian; Dax gave a countdown from five with her fingers, then depressed the trigger. She was wide by about a half meter—*not bad,* she thought—and she swept the phaser beam sideways to brush both her targets before either could draw a weapon or get off a communication to the planetary command. She made sure that she fired at a slight downward angle, striking the Cardassians about knee high . . . both to avoid the battle armor on their torsos and to make sure the phaser beam grounded into the dirt rather than flashed across the sky like a beacon.

She didn't look over at Julian's targets until her own were down, so she didn't know how precise he had been, but all four Cardassians were stunned into unconsciousness. Jadzia cautiously led the doctor the last hundred meters; while she scanned for approaching enemies, Julian examined the Cardassians, gave medical treatment to one who had injured himself falling, and then injected all four with the stasis sedative. "Its purpose," he explained, as he worked the hypospray, "is to stabilize an injured patient for transport to a medical facility; I'm sure they'll be all right." His voice didn't sound as certain as his words, but frankly, Dax cared little about how safe the Cardassians might be: she had seen them mow down women, children, and old folks without a second thought in the battle of Tiffnaki.

Nobody showed up. Dax and the doctor bundled

the Cardassians into the large skimmer, splashed liquor all over the soldiers and the interior of the vehicle, and sent it on a wild ride across the fruited plain at maximum speed, veering wildly and careening up and over hills and through passes. As the driverless car took off and accelerated, Jadzia Dax couldn't help throwing them a salute; the program was set to erase itself shortly before landing . . . not a trace would remain of two Federation agents on Sierra-Bravo.

They stocked up on Cardassian food, unpleasant tasting but edible, and hopped aboard the remaining skimmer, a cycle that normally seated only one. Dax insisted upon driving, with a dubious and nervous Julian hanging on behind. "Point me in the right direction and look out," she yelled, firing up the noisy engines. "I was born to ride!"

Joson Wabak tried not to let it show, but his frustration was rising like a core breach; having a conversation by *radio waves,* of all the primitive things, with a sea monster was like . . . *It's not like anything!* he concluded; *they never taught us anything about this sort of situation at the Academy.* In a dark recess of his mind, Joson was already composing the strongly worded letter to the Chief of Starfleet Education and Training, Captain Bruchenheimer, about the need for more sea-monster simulation training for upperclassmen.

"Weymouth, give me a rundown."

"Nothing's changed since last time, sir."

"Just the rundown, Ensign—not an editorial aside!"

Tina cringed a little, but Joson was getting tired of her attitude. "The, ah, sea monster doesn't have a name; it thinks we're an egg from another like itself; it thinks we're about to hatch—something about the way we taste, from what little the not-so-universal translator can translate—and it wants to help us. We've convinced it to hold off, that cracking us open would prevent our character growth or something, and we're currently trying to make it understand that we need to get to the surface—but it doesn't get it."

"That is to be expected," said Ensign N'Kduk-Thag. "If this creature were to ascend to the surface it probably could not survive the light and low pressure. Perhaps it thinks we are confused and wants to protect us."

"Well, we'd better do something quick, Joson." Tina hunched over her console, staring at a gauge. "We're down to a containment-field strength of seventeen percent. The hull could rupture any moment—Below twenty percent, there's a measurable chance every minute of a sudden, catastrophic collapse of the containment field, the hull, and all the contents . . . what they kind of quaintly refer to as a 'phase-change singularity' in the manual."

"The ensign is quite correct," confirmed Ensign Nick. "We must ascend immediately at least five hundred meters."

"Open the channel again," said Joson, rubbing his tired eyes. *At least it's an audio-only broadcast,* he thought; *I'm not sure she could deal with creatures that look like us actually talking to her in her own language.*

Weymouth hissed to get his attention, then nodded; Joson Wabak began to speak.

"*Defiant,* speaking to our friend. You must release us and allow us to continue toward the surface. We will not be harmed! Our . . . mother lives near the surface; it's where we come from."

He waited, but the monster didn't respond; one of the frustating things about the conversation was the long lag time between their transmission and the response . . . evidently, the sheer size of the sea monster's nervous system made for slow, deep, sluggish thoughts.

"Let us ascend," added Joson. "Our—shell is too fragile to survive at this depth. We need a lower pressure, or our shell will crack, um, prematurely." *Great, I wonder whether she's getting ANY of this?* It seemed unlikely; Joson wasn't an engineer and didn't exactly know how the universal translator worked, but he knew all it could do was form "word pictures" that would be translated by the receiver's own brain into language . . . assuming the two brains weren't too dissimilar. It was hard to imagine two more dissimilar brains than his own and that of a two-kilometer-wide sea monster who lived a thousand meters deep in an inky-black ocean. The vast majority of concepts that a surface dweller such as himself took for granted—sunlight, color, the sky, air!—would be so utterly alien to her, how could she possibly understand a word he said?

We might just be fooling ourselves. He caught Ensign Weymouth's eye and ran his finger across his throat; she closed the transmission channel . . . all they could do now was wait for the Old Girl to respond.

And she was old, too. N'Kduk-Thag occupied himself scanning the creature, integrating the holoscan information from the abortive probe they had launched earlier. "I believe this creature is at least thirty thousand years old," he announced out of the blue.

"Why?" asked Joson. "What makes you say that?"

"I carbon-dated deposits found on the inside of the entity's intestines."

"Maybe she ate some old rocks."

"Joson," said Tina with a smile, "thirty thousand years would be incredibly *young* for a rock."

"I believe the deposits were produced by organic material ingested by the creature. There are deposits of every age up to approximately thirty thousand years but none older than that age."

Joson shrugged, watching the maw of the sea monster open and close on the forward viewer. "Well, no wonder she takes so long to answer."

"Sir . . . Joson, we haven't got much time."

He settled back, closing his eyes. "We haven't got much we can do, either, Tina."

"A full barrage of photon torpedoes will at least get the creature's attention. It might be surprised into letting us go."

"Or it might get mad and crush us! Nick, no torpedoes . . . not unless *I* order it." Ensign Joson Wabak, acting captain, opened his eyes and sat up straight again. "Look, Dax left *me* in charge, and unless things change drastically—"

The ship lurched abruptly, knocking the enlisted security crew to the deck. The three officers managed to keep their seats, but only barely. Weymouth grabbed the edge of her console to steady herself until the stabilizers could catch up with the unexpected movement. "Jesus, Joson! She's dragging us *into her mouth!*"

Ensign N'Kduk-Thag emotionlessly played his fingers across his own station. "Photon torpedoes armed and ready for your command, sir."

"Belay those torpedoes!" hollered Wabak, staring at the forward viewer. Something was strange, different, something he couldn't quite . . . "The tongues!" he exclaimed. "Look at the tongues!"

"What? What?" Tina sounded confused, panicky. "What about the tongues? They're not doing anything!"

"Exactly . . . they're not doing anything!" Nobody responded; Ensigns Nick and Weymouth stared at him without comprehension. "Don't you get it, guys? It's swallowing us whole . . . it's not *chewing* us!"

"This is your last opportunity to fire the torpedoes. After this point we shall be too close for safe operation."

"Stand down the torpedoes, Nick. That's an order."

Unemotional to the end, N'Kduk-Thag turned back to his weapons board and disarmed the torpedoes. The maw loomed closer, soon filling the entire viewer. Behind Joson, the enlisted man with the mustache started shouting: "Sir, do something! *It's swallowing us!*"

"Shut him up, now!" snapped Wabak; he heard the chief hushing her terrified third-class, then he tuned the pair of them out. "Tina! Hull integrity!"

"Dropping, down to fifteen percent, but—"

"Hull pressure?" *Please,* he begged the Prophets, hoping they could hear his prayer so far away, so deep beneath the waves, *please let my hunch be right!*

"Hull pressure is . . ." Ensign Weymouth faded into silence, then cleared her throat and continued. "Hull pressure is dropping," she said in a small voice, "down to sixty atmospheres . . . fifty-five."

Ensign N'Kduk-Thag slid across to the science console and began a level-two scan. "The creature has closed its mouth and is expanding its alimentary cavity. The increased volume is resulting in a drop in the atmospheric pressure on the hull."

Joson breathed a sigh of relief. "She's not eating us. She's . . . *carrying* us." Ensign Wabak was struck by a sudden worry. "Nick, what's happening to the antenna?"

"The antenna is trailing behind us but I cannot determine whether it extends outside the creature's mouth or has been severed. In any event it should still be usable though it may not be long enough to reach the surface of the ocean."

"Can we still talk to her?"

"The radio channel is still open," said Tina, seeming to have recovered her wits. "The carrier signal sounds the same; I suppose it still works."

Weymouth continued to call the numbers; the atmospheric pressure of the seawater surrounding the *Defiant* continued to drop, finally leveling out at approximately fifteen atmospheres. The crew proceeded with emergency repairs to the containment field, which they were able to turn off: the hull itself could withstand that much pressure for a brief period without significant damage.

"Sir, we appear to be ascending," said N'Kduk-Thag, still seated at the panel usually occupied by Commander Dax, the science officer, when the ship had a full crew complement. "We have risen to a depth of seven hundred twenty meters we are ascending approximately twenty meters per minute."

Suddenly, Joson Wabak felt a terrible fatigue. He collapsed back in the captain's chair, shivering from the suddenly chilly air on his sweat-drenched uniform. Ensign Weymouth interrupted his relief: "Joson, it's the sea monster. She's asking if we're feeling better—and asking where we want her to take us. At least, I *think* that's what she's saying . . . the translation isn't particularly clear."

"Nick, can you track the runabout that Commander Dax and Doctor Bashir took up?"

After a moment, N'Kduk-Thag responded. "The crushed debris from the runabout lie at the bottom of the ocean approximately ten kilometers on a bearing of two-thirteen. There is no evidence of human or Trill remains."

Prophets guide them . . . I hope they made it safely! "They were heading toward the land mass. Tina, open the channel." Joson waited for her nod. "*Defiant* to sea monster. Our health is improving. We are grateful to you. We wish to be placed near the shoreline, but if you cannot ascend that high, let us go at as shallow a depth as you can tolerate." He gestured, and Weymouth cut the jury-rigged radio transmitter.

"We should remain somewhat underwater for cover," suggested Ensign Nick. Joson nodded, distracted by his own thoughts—the watery grave they had almost shared with the *Amazon*.

There was no further communication from the sea monster. Twenty minutes later, she gently disgorged the "egg" at a depth of somewhat less than four hundred meters. The pressure increased slowly as she contracted her "stomach," rising to a high but manageable thirty-eight atmospheres of pressure. The patched containment field rode steadily at seventy-four percent, and the *Defiant* continued her climb up the underwater slope until she rested only seventy meters deep at the edge of the continental shelf, which towered above them to within ten meters of the surface. A runabout trip from their present position to the shore itself would be simple and safe . . . *that is,* thought the ensign, *unless the Cardies catch us.*

"Extend what's left of the floating antenna, N'Kduk-Thag. We'll sit here and wait for the commander to call us. I don't want to take any chances with the spoon—with the Cardassians. In the meantime . . ." Joson gestured vaguely. "Go get some sleep, everyone. I'll be in the captain's ready room."

Exhausted, the bridge crew stumbled toward the turbolift, while Joson Wabak wondered whether he would make it all the way to the bed before collapsing into a deep and dream-troubled sleep.

CHAPTER 11

MAJOR KIRA NERYS walked unsteadily toward the turbolift; the last sight she saw before the platform disappeared below the deck of the Ops level was Kai Winn on her "widow's walk" balcony overlooking the prime-team of combat technicians. The middle-aged woman, far from looking haggard, was serene, as if she had taken a full night's sleep instead of the four hours of Kira's watch as CDO, Command Duty Officer. Then the turbolift picked up speed, rushing Kira down to the Promenade, then along one of the crossover tunnels to her own quarters.

The aliens had shifted to a waiting game. Their ships still surrounded the *Emissary's Sanctuary,* what once had been called *Deep Space Nine* (and

Terok Nor before that), but the shattered ruins of eight Bajoran cruisers testified to the inability of Bajor to come to the station's aid. Kai Winn had issued orders, with First Minister Shakar's concurrence, that the heavier ships still in dry dock be completed with all deliberate speed . . . but that would take at least two weeks, and Kira personally doubted the station could withstand a siege of that length. Sooner or later, the aliens—whoever they were—would find a weak point and burst inside.

Maybe they'll run when they see the new Freedom-class starships, the major consoled herself, walking around the habitat ring to her door. *Maybe they'll just get tired and go away.* She smiled. *Maybe the Prophets will put in an appearance and smite them with lightning from the wormhole.* The possibilities seemed equally unlikely.

Shaking from fatigue and too much watchfulness, Kira lay faceup on her rack, dimming the lights but not killing them entirely. Then she remembered the message she had gotten out . . . despite the Kai's orders, again seconded by Shakar (to Kira's dismay), not to ask the Federation for help, Kira had fired off a heavily encrypted subspace message to a Bajoran friend of hers in Starfleet, a former Resistance fighter in another cell she trusted utterly. Two days had passed, long enough for the fleet to receive the forwarded subspace message and reply.

She rose painfully and limped to her computer console. Working entirely by touch, saying nothing aloud—she wasn't sure why, but it seemed appropriate—Kira found the incoming message and displayed it with the sound muted.

She saw her friend, Bel Anar, and he looked terrible. *Probably as bad as I looked,* she thought grimly. He had clearly been in combat for several hours. His lips moved, and Kira read the subtitles supplied by the computer in the absence of audio.

> Got your message, Nerys. The Kai, may the Prophets bless her, has officially told the Council that she *doesn't* want any help. Hang on . . . don't let them kill you! FleetIntel says they're not Cardassians and nobody's ever seen that ship design—probably not Dominion, but who knows. Starfleet will be keeping an eye on the situation. Prophets bless you, my sister-in-arms. Good luck.

With downcast eyes, Anar terminated the message.

Shaking her head in frustration, Kira deleted the message using a security override that she was pretty sure the Kai couldn't break. Since her attempt at circumventing Kai Winn's isolationism had failed, she sure as hell didn't want the Kai to find out she had tried.

Kira had just padded back to the bed and laid herself down to sleep when the door chirped. "Computer, who is it?" she asked.

"Jake Sisko," said the melodious voice.

"Come," she said, rising up to a seated position. She heard the door hiss open and footsteps enter; there was a bang, followed by soft cursing. "Lights three-quarters normal," said Kira belatedly.

Blinking in the sudden illumination, Kira walked into the living room of her two-room suite. Jake was rubbing his shin and staring disgustedly at the Bajoran "primitive period" tea table. "Where did you get that stupid thing?" he demanded.

"It was a gift from Shakar," said Kira, actually enjoying seeing the young man squirm in embarrassment.

"Uh . . . sorry. It's, um, really nice."

"I'm trying to sleep, Jake."

"Oh! I can come back in a couple of hours if you're—"

"Just tell me what you want!"

Jake stood as tall as his father, but probably carried only two thirds the muscle mass; Kira couldn't help seeing him as she had the first day they arrived at the station, newly liberated from the Cardassians: the superimposition of a young boy over a young man's figure was eerie. *I'm just tired,* she decided.

"I . . ." Jake paused, collecting his thoughts. "I want to join the defense militia."

Kira raised her eyebrows; for more than a year, Jake had been acting strangely—sometimes taking wild, unnecessary chances, then seemingly afraid of his own shadow. "So? Why come to me? Kai Winn organized the militia herself."

"That's just the point!" exclaimed Jake. "She's only allowing Bajorans to fight!"

Ah, the sting of offering to help and being ignored. Get used to it, kid; welcome to the universe. "Jake, it's her station and her militia. Why do you want to join anyway? You're not a soldier."

"They won't let Garak join, either!"

"Hah! Well, what a shock. Kai Winn doesn't want a Cardassian in the Bajoran militia? Outrageous!"

"Well, you don't have to get sarcastic about it." Jake sat sullenly on Kira's couch.

She felt bad; Jake, at least, seemed sincere in his desire to protect the station. (She was never so sure about Garak, tailor to the Obsidian Order.) "Look, I'm tired; I shouldn't have made fun. Jake, there are two problems here: first, like it or not, this is a *Bajoran station* now. The captain's not in charge anymore . . . and I don't have a lot of influence over the Kai, no matter that she seems to like me for some strange reason."

"I just thought maybe you could—"

"And *second,* you are the Emissary's son! Even if Kai Winn were accepting nonBajorans, she'd probably invite *Garak* before she would invite you . . . you still don't realize what your father means to us! The Kai would never take the slightest chance of angering him by putting you in harm's way."

"But—but how can I look Dad in the eye if I don't do my part?" His voice sounded hollow, defeated, as if he saw a chance to prove, well, something slipping away like a spring deer into the woods. "How can I look at myself in the mirror?"

"You can't look either of you in the eye if you're dead, Jake."

Jake's face fell; it was finally sinking in that whatever he needed to prove to himself, he wasn't going to be given the chance. Not this time. Jake rose and left with a mumbled goodbye.

Kira felt terrible; she had been younger than Jake when she began fighting for the Resistance. She knew exactly what he felt . . . the burning need to *do something,* to stand up for what was right. But Bajor was desperate and needed anyone who could hold a gun or plant a bomb; at this point, thank the Prophets, *Emissary's Sanctuary* was still holding its own against the unknown raiders; traditional rules that were broken during the Occupation would be more rigidly enforced.

Kira drifted back to her rack, wondering who would be next to disturb her five hours of alleged rest.

It was, surprisingly, Garak the alleged tailor. This time, Kira had not so much as closed her eyes before the door chirped, sounding somehow polite and imperious at once. "Why not?" asked the major aloud; the computer did not recognize that as an answer and chirped again; this time, Major Kira said the customary.

"Garak," she said through clenched teeth, "*what* do you want now?"

"Now? My dear Major Kira, I have asked for

nothing, *nothing,* during this entire dreadful siege!" The Cardassian tried to look blameless but succeeded only in a smug, condescending expression.

"But you have something now. Right?" Kira was beyond weariness, painfully aware that Garak was allowed to remain on the Bajoran station only because there literally was nowhere else for him to go, but the Cardassian, not surprisingly, had been the target of countless curses, epithets, and even a few violent assaults since the turnover. He had some claim to victimhood . . . *a LITTLE claim,* she amended, thinking of who he had once been.

"I understand," said Garak with a smile, "that the tiny, inadequate Bajoran fleet floats in ruins near the station and that the Federation will not send aid so long as Kai Winn refuses to ask for it."

Kira could not help staring. "How the hell did you know that?"

Garak fluttered his hands, a dismissive gesture. "Oh, I like to keep in touch. The point is, the raiders haven't left . . . which means they, too, know that they are in no immediate danger."

Kira said nothing, merely stared coldly, waiting for the former member of the Cardassian Obsidian Order to get to the point.

"And the fact that they've stopped their ineffectual shooting," he said, "implies that they're working on something more significant, a siege engine, to use an ancient term. Do you understand what I'm saying?"

"You haven't said anything worth hearing yet."

Garak shook his head. "So impatient. No wonder you were so easy to conquer." The major resisted the temptation to push her fist through Garak's smug teeth. "Major Kira, there comes a time when the best defense is to fold up one's tent and steal away."

Kira was tired, but not too tired to catch the drift. "You're suggesting that we surrender the station to these scum?"

"To these very enterprising scum who hold *for the moment* a decisive military advantage."

"They're just sitting out there! They're not doing anything."

"They are sitting out there . . . but I would be willing to bet my auto-hemmer that they *are* doing something. Major Kira, if we wait until their next attack, we may not be given the option of surrender. They have not made any attempt to communicate with you or respond to your own communications, is that not so?"

"You seem unusually well informed about our secrets. You tell me."

"I don't think it's because they can't hear you; it's far more likely they don't care to listen. But if you offer them something worthwhile to listen to . . ."

"Terms of surrender?"

Garak shrugged. "If you will. Perhaps that will catch their attention. You could evacuate the station, and all our lives would be spared."

"You mean *your* life would be spared. I doubt you care much about the rest of us. . . ."

"Kira! You malign me. Think instead of the Bajorans on the station. Have you thought, perhaps, that only your own stubbornness and pride are preventing you from saving all those Bajoran lives?"

"And handing over the station to raiders from the Gamma Quadrant, for them to launch attacks on Bajor itself! No thank you, Garak. Good night."

The tailor spread his hands, shaking his head. "Major, Major, who but you and the Kai would be in a better position to sabotage every system on *Deep Space Nine?* Oh, I beg your pardon . . . *Emissary's Sanctuary;* or is it back to being *Terok Nor?* I never can keep those names straight."

"Sabotage the station?"

"Bajor would lose the high ground, but at least these raiders would have nothing to show for their audacity. We should never think of rewarding criminal actions."

Kira stood. "Good *night,* Garak. This station will never be surrendered."

"You will at least discuss my suggestion with your superior?"

"Good-bye!" Major Kira thumbed the door open and firmly pointed at the corridor beyond. Garak sighed deeply, as a man much misjudged and chivvied by the entire universe; then he skulked through the doorway and strode away, probably to plant more seeds of doubt in the minds of frightened, vulnerable Bajoran civilians. *Well, he won't find us so easy to manipulate,* she thought decisively—wondering whether it were true or merely a salving boast.

At last, she was left alone, but she could not fall asleep. One thing only that Garak had said stuck with her: no one currently on board knew as much about the station systems and subsystems as Kira Nerys . . . and if the worst came to pass, and the station lost the siege and was conquered (she did not think for a moment it would ever be surrendered), could she allow these faceless raiders to get hold of such a powerful weapon? On the other hand, surely Kai Winn would never allow Kira to sabotage the station in advance! That would be seen as defeatist, and possibly undermining their defense.

Kira made a decision: she would set in motion a series of computer programs—viruses, actually—that could be activated in a few minutes and would shut down everything that could be shut down . . . permanently. And she would not tell the Kai; it would be Kira's own little secret.

But what if Kira herself died in the defense, as was likely? *Better yet,* she amended, *the viruses will require a code word from me NOT to activate automatically.* It was popularly called a "deadman switch"; unless Kira spoke her code word at regular intervals, the sabotage would proceed all by itself, and the raiders would never know what hit them. It was a dangerous move: if Kira died or became incapacitated before the station surrendered, the autosabotage would end any prayer the *Emissary's Sanctuary* had of surviving. But the alternative—quantum torpedoes raining down upon Bajoran cities—was too horrible to contemplate.

Nervous, unable to stop her mind from racing, Kira rolled and thrashed on her bed, readjusting the temperature and calling for soothing music and ocean noises in a fruitless attempt to get some sleep. At some point, she drifted off into a nightmare-filled doze, but it was not restful. When the alarm sounded, alerting her to her next shift, she felt as if she had spent the night wrestling with a particularly slippery *vole* in the pay of the Obsidian Order. She wasn't sure which of them had won the match.

"Good afternoon, child," said Kai Winn as her young protegee rose on the turbolift; Nerys looked haggard and bitter; *is that how she looked during the Occupation?* wondered the Kai. *It's almost funny . . . one of my DUTIES was to look as fresh as the morning dew. My flock wanted to look at their Sister and see hope, not despair.* The hard-bitten Resistance fighters may never have realized how much easier a job they had than the secret spies, the deep-cover operatives, who had no infrastructure, no weapons but their wits, no bolt-hole for flight if everything went wrong. *And WE had to do it with a smile.*

Kai Winn smiled now, just as she had so many years ago, lending hope in an even more hopeless situation. It wouldn't be fair to deprive Major Kira of the security she so desperately needed, the reassurance that everything was going to be all right. *She needs serenity; I must be serene, no matter what I feel. I must be the wings of peace enfolding her—and the rest of my flock on this station.*

"What's so good about it?" snapped Nerys, glowering all the harder at the Kai's smile; but Winn knew that deep inside, Nerys was grateful as a child reassured by her mother.

"We are alive, child, and we still walk with the Prophets. What could be better?"

"We may be about to die!"

"Everyone dies, Nerys. Be thankful you've lived as long as you have and played such a role in the great events of history."

Major Kira said nothing, her mouth contorting in an effort to remain grumpy. She took a cup of *ratageena* from the replicator and hovered over the shoulders of the Kai's combat team, checking the situation (and obviously snubbing Winn upon her balcony). "I will retire now," said the Kai. Nerys looked up then, her face vulnerable, frightened for a moment; then she hardened into *Major Kira* again, nodding curtly.

Kai Winn stepped inside her quarters, what once had been the Emissary's office—it still smelled of His Holiness; she stepped more lightly and gracefully than her heavy heart truly felt . . . perhaps a lie, but a necessary lie. She knew and dreaded what awaited her: for reasons known only to Themselves, the Prophets had chosen this moment for Kai Winn to relive her days under the Occupation in her dreams, and she could not deny those dreams. She must face them and try to learn from them what lessons the Prophets taught.

She thought of delaying her sleep, returning to Ops and telling Nerys in detail everything that hadn't happened while the poor girl had been trying to sleep, but it would just be an evasion of the inevitable. The major would read the log; she would note that the unknown raiders had crept slowly closer, perhaps believing their movement was not detected. Nerys was a good leader, even at such a tender age, on all such routine matters . . . though she knew nothing as yet of the subtle interplay between personality and policy that she would learn, over time, from the mentor she didn't even know she had. *It will be a blessing on her to teach her the art of politics,* thought Winn with a smile. *How else will she hold her own with her chosen, First Minister Shakar?*

Sighing, her heart already starting to pound and her forehead already damp, Winn lay on her rack and tried to wet her lips. She was afraid her old body might not cooperate, keeping her awake despite her resolve, but the Prophets knew what They wanted. She blinked twice, and found herself standing again on Surface 92, the long, straight, Cardassian road leading from one world to the next.

The dream started again. . . .

CHAPTER 12

THIRTY YEARS AGO

Riis! thought Sister Winn, as the column crested the last rise of Surface 92 before descending into the river valley that held the town.

Riis, the mighty "hand" on the rolling Shakiristi River, where four other tributaries joined and swelled the Shakiristi to a three-kilometers-wide forearm thrusting between the Granite Prayers and Lakastor mountain ranges to the Cold Sea. Riis extended its fingers up each of the four tributaries and the thick Shakiristi itself, and downstream an additional kilometer, the wrist of Riis.

The Riis docks handled more cargo than any other city west of the Granite Prayers, its spaceport often called the Palm of Bajor. But for all that activity, it was still a quiet, quaint old city compared to other industrial giants. There were suburbs but no urban centers, not as Sister Winn understood the term; jobs were plentiful, and the crime rate was noticeably lower than in the wild mining cities near where Winn had grown up. By a trick of the weather, a gentle breeze blew often across Riis, not only cooling the city but blowing away (into nearby North Riisil) the inevitable by-products of an industrial civilization: smog and soot. (Once every few months, there was instead a stiff back-breeze from the north, sending the pollutants back where they came from redoubled; natives of Riis called such a wind "Riisil's Revenge.")

Riis, Winn remembered, was said to have been founded three thousand years earlier, when a holy man named Kilikarri went fishing in the Shakiristi, cast his net, and miraculously caught not only a hundred fish but the third Scroll of Prophecy, written in jet-black letters on a golden parchment. The scroll was supposed to be on display in the vault of the Temple of the Emissary Kilikarri, but a newly minted sister was not likely to be admitted by the temple preceptors or the father vedek.

As Gul Ragat's household descended into Riis, the sun was newly risen, bathing the slumbering city in a golden red glow through the cloud cover. A permanent rainbow arced across the Palm of Bajor as a gentle mist rose from the rapids; the mist fell as a drizzle, and when the corner of water reached the column, Sister Winn said a grateful prayer to the Prophets for their cooling touch—which she chose to interpret as a sign that she wasn't straying from her duty, that all would work out well, that she wouldn't end up accidentally betraying the Resistance and getting a whole cell captured.

Surface 92 led directly into the outskirts of Riis, but there it ended abruptly where the jurisdiction of the Cardassian civil engineers had run into the military jurisdiction of the governor of the prefecture. The caravan had made excellent time; it was barely two hours past sunrise—and still many hours before the actual planned time of the strike at the spaceport, which would come at sundown, just before the changing of the Cardassian sentries. *The Prophets,* thought Sister Winn, *I hope will forgive me my lie to Gul Ragat.*

The Shakiristi River was so important to Riis (and Riis to the river) that the city extended itself right into the water; many "streets" in Riis were waterways, plied by motorboats and even a few that were rowed. "Sidewalks" floated upon the water, making a journey by foot perilous through parts of the city, especially for priestesses who had never spent time on boats or at sea.

The Cardassians on their skimmers (one pair riding double) were unaffected by the rocking, heaving sidewalks, of course, and even Gul Ragat seemed oblivious to the difficulty his Bajoran servants had; the household had to trot briskly to keep up with the impatient gul, and a maid and a skimmer mechanic slipped on the supposedly non-skid surface of a floating sidewalk and took an unexpected swim together. Hersaaka Toos, the Bajoran overseer, fished them out; Winn made sure neither was hurt before hurrying after her "master."

The Heavenward Prayer Spaceport—now charmingly renamed Collection Point One—stood not in the center of Riis but on the outskirts, dating from a time when space travel was unfamiliar and frightening to many Bajorans and the farmers demanded that rocket-based ships not fly over their land. Gul Ragat decided his mob would lurk in the town until close to the moment of the expected raid, so they wouldn't scare the "rebels" away.

He stopped his limousine skimmer and stepped out to speak to Sister Winn. "You said the attack would come this morning . . . late morning. Before noon, surely?" The eagerness shone from his eyes; Gul Ragat was dazzled by visions of his own glory, his ascension to the full governorship—the youngest governor on Bajor!—and perhaps an early promotion to legate. Young though Winn felt, she knew she was older than the gul, and not just chronologically.

"I said it *may come* as early as this morning, My Lord. They could easily hold off until the afternoon if there were problems, or even until nightfall, to take best advantage of the darkness." In fact, the raid was meticulously planned. "But please, My Lord . . . are you *sure* I'm doing the right thing? I feel so very like a—a betrayer!"

She stared anxiously at Gul Ragat and allowed

him to reassure her that ratting out her own people was in fact the very best thing she could do. *Can't appear too eager,* she warned herself. The gul didn't look at her as he spoke; he stared around him at the people walking across the huge, floating merchants' square, probably wondering which of them was an agent of the Resistance. Sister Winn wondered the same; she was not from Riis, had been to Riis only twice, and knew none of the cell members or protocols—of course! The whole point of a cell structure was to minimize the damage if one should turn or be captured and tortured: what you didn't know, you couldn't spill, no matter what the reason.

Gul Ragat was a child in a sweetshop, staring at everything with big round eyes. He had never before involved himself in the counter-Resistance, never felt the quickening of his pulse, the dizziness of anxiety, wondering whether he would give himself away and frighten the rebels away . . . or even be assassinated. Winn watched him openly, since he was not looking at her; he shrank suddenly into the shadows, drawing his coat closer about his shoulders, though the day was heating up with the rising sun. Gul Ragat had abruptly realized how vulnerable he was . . . a young gul with only sixteen guards in a city admittedly crawling with Resistance fighters!

Winn felt a malignant presence behind her; turning, she saw Neemak Counselor. He pushed past her without a glance and approached the gul, speaking in low tones that she could not hear. She didn't need to; she knew what he was saying: he grew suspicious at the gul's behavior; the counselor desperately wanted to figure out what Ragat planned so Neemak could report it to his true superior. But the gul knew the game, at least in theory, and would keep his own counsel, even from his counselor. In Gul Ragat's fantasy, when the smoke cleared, who was to say that he hadn't simply been in the right place at the right time and shown proper, Cardassian initiative to thwart a damaging rebel attack?

Winn, however, had her own designs. She eyeballed the square, watching citizens step aboard, conduct their business, and step off. She, the gul, and Neemak hovered in the shadow of a teahouse that also served food, and the smell was almost holy after two days of traveler's rations. But Ragat was much too excited to think of eating, and it was not Winn's place to suggest it. In any event, she was intent upon finding someone she recognized and getting a message out somehow; the smell and the sizzle of breakfast was just a distraction.

The Prophets finally heard the priestess's prayer. A young man—still a boy, actually—stepped across the gap between the floating sidewalk and the merchants' square; she recognized him as Barada Vai, whose older sister, Barada Mirina, was a prospect for Winn's own Resistance cell some months back. "Prospect" was probably too lofty a term; the priestess's ears reddened at the thought that the girl was more than likely an "anybody's," passed around from man to man in the cell. In any event, Sister Winn had met the Barada family, and Vai might well remember her; a visit from a sister or brother was an important social event in a traditional Bajoran family.

But how can I talk to him without Ragat panicking? She stared hungrily at the boy, aware that she had only a few moments before he finished purchasing whatever he came to buy and hopped across to the sidewalk again. *Think fast!* she commanded. *There is your brother, within an easy shout or a couple of long steps . . . do something!*

It was as if the Prophets Themselves suddenly whispered into Winn's ear, so swiftly did the plan form. She gasped with the wonder of it, and the gul heard her, but that was fine, it fit well with the scheme.

"My Lord," she whispered, "this is . . . this is dreadful!"

"What is? What's happened?" The gul was already jumpy; now he grew quite agitated, worried that his opportunity might slip through his fingers.

"That boy there . . . he's my brother!"

"Your brother? Your real brother?"

"My half brother on my father's side," said the priestess in agony, "and—and he must be working at the spaceport!"

"The spaceport? Wait, didn't you know?"

She turned to the gul, trying as hard as she could to blanch. "No, no! How could I have known? I haven't seen him for three years! But he wrote to my father and told him he had gotten a job at a spaceport, for he's always wanted to be a pilot . . . but I didn't know where. But if he's here, at Riis, then he's—My Lord, he'll be directly in the line of fire! He may be killed! Oh master, I beg of you, spare this boy's life—he's no Resistance fighter!"

"Hush!" ordered Ragat, aghast at her indiscretion. "Keep your voice down, I *order* you!" He looked fearfully where Neemak had been but a moment before, but the shifty counselor had slithered away, as he often did without asking leave. This time, as with many others, the gul looked relieved rather than affronted.

"Please, My Lord, let me warn the boy . . . let him be away from that place when your lordship springs his surprise."

"Sister Winn, you can't warn him of my trap! What can you be thinking? He'll run straight to the rebels, whether he's in the Resistance or not."

"He won't!"

Gul Ragat rolled his eyes. "Any Bajoran boy would." He considered a long moment; he liked to think of himself as a compassionate man, and Sister Winn was one of his favorites. "This far will I let you: you may tell some plausible lie to keep him away from his job for today, but we will work it out now, and you *will not deviate* from the script." He lowered his brows and tried to look menacing, a task quite easy for a Cardassian; his scowl shook Winn and scared her. "I would not like to have to arrest you on a charge of aiding the rebellion against rightful authority."

She inclined her head submissively. "My Lord," she agreed. "Shall I . . . tell him you need him to—take holos of some event you're sponsoring? A banquet, perhaps?"

"Yes, that might—wait, a party; my birthday party."

"Is it your birthday, My Lord?"

"No, there's no birthday, but there's no party, either! A perfect match. Yes, that will do. Let's go to him and get it over with; I don't like standing in the middle of the square attracting attention."

Winn had hoped to get a chance to talk to the boy alone, but that was a silly thought. For all that Gul Ragat thought of himself as a kind, gentle master, he was still a Cardassian untroubled by the thought of owning slaves. With so much at stake, he would not allow one slave to conspire with another outside his hearing!

The pair approached Barada Vai, and Sister Winn attempted to feel as serene as she looked; like all priests, she had learned to wear the mask: it was necessary when comforting the dying, for example. But sometimes, the mask crept inward, and this was one of those times. With every step, Winn's certainty increased that the lad would not blow the game.

"Barada Vai," said Ragat, "you recognize this woman, do you not?"

Vai looked at Winn's habit, recognizing its clerical significance but no more. "A sister," he said uncertainly.

Winn smiled broadly. "Has it been so long, my brother? You were so much younger when I left home, but I'm your sister, Winn. Didn't mother tell you I was to take holy orders?"

Barada Vai froze for a moment; then the natural guile of youth took over, and he fell very naturally into the game, swiftly aware that they were playing a joke on a hated Cardassian. "Sis!" he cried, his entire face suddenly breaking into a grin. "I didn't recognize you . . ."

"Vai-lak, you may trust this fine lord *completely.* He is truly a prince among Cardassians, a natural master, and he treats well those of us marked by nature to be subservient. He has an important task for you." Winn worried she might be laying it on a bit thick, but Ragat was too busy preening to realize what any other Bajoran would understand, that Winn was really saying: "Don't believe a word the son of a bachelor says!"

She was about to explain about the holos, but Gul Ragat seized control of the conversation. "Lad, I have an important task for you. Your sister says you are handy with a holocam; I need holos taken of my birthday celebration today. You will return home and get your holocam, then run to . . ." The gul trailed off, evidently not familiar enough with the floating city of Riis to suggest a location.

"To the Hall of the Legion of Prophets," supplied Sister Winn smoothly; every large Bajoran city had one.

"I'm sorry," added Ragat, "but you can't go to the spaceport today."

"The—spaceport?" asked Barada Vai, suddenly puzzled.

Winn interjected smoothly, confident the Prophets would whisper into the boy's ear. "Your job there is important, I know, but you *cannot be there* today. There is something much more important to do: the holos are important; *the holos are very, very important.* Much more important than whatever trivial task you perform at your job at the spaceport." She snuck a glance at Ragat to see if he had noticed the special emphasis she placed on the holos; he seemed thoughtful, and she felt a tendril of fear. But she pressed on; a priestess could not allow fear to override duty.

Ragat took control of the conversation again; his tone indicated some distress, perhaps the intimation that something had been passed . . . but he could not place his bony, Cardassian finger on it. "Be at the, ah, Hall of the Legion of Prophets within the hour, and *wait there* until I or my men arrive. Do you understand the order?"

"Yes, My Lord," said Barada Vai, all earnest eyes and nodding chin. Dismissed, he sped away, carrying Sister Winn's hopes with him.

She had confidence that he would figure out at least the overt part of the warning: *Don't go to the spaceport!* was clear enough. If the boy had maintained his connections to the Resistance, he would promptly report the unusual command, even if he had no knowledge of the raid. *But will he comprehend the second, deeper message?* wondered the priestess. The words that had fretted at Gul Ragat, "the holos are very, very important," were the heart of Winn's own mission . . . which indeed was more important than a trivial raid on a spaceport. Sister Winn's holos, still lodged semisecurely in her trick boot heel, contained the key to Cardassian military codes, plans, and bases that would lend solid effectiveness to the Resistance for years to come, if used cautiously. And everything now rested in the capricious understanding of a child barely past puberty whose connection with the movement was less than savory.

Gul Ragat stepped away from the publicity of the floating market square toward the landed portion of Riis, there to resume his vigil for intelligence of the raid. He did not even glance back to see that Winn followed . . . which she did meekly, never having given cause for Cardassian offense. He seemed to have left off pondering the weight of her words about the holos; her cover, she decided, was still intact.

For how much longer? wondered the priestess, having the first, faint intimations that she might be on her last mission, even if successful. If the Obsidian Order ever realized how they had been compromised, an investigation would commence the likes of which had rarely been seen on Bajor. The legate would probably be withdrawn; and chance encounters, recalled, such as Winn's brush with the guard in the code room. The priestess would have little in her future but a tortuous trial and torturous detention on *Terok Nor,* in the loving ministration of Gul Dukat, assuming she were allowed to live that long.

She swallowed, stumbling on the heaving sidewalk behind her "master." The consolation would be the utter ruin of the young Gul Ragat before her and of his smug acceptance of his own superiority . . . and this time, Sister Winn did not even apologize to the Prophets for her uncharity! She still reveled in the image.

PRESENT DAY

Eyes downcast, trying his best to look humbled and shaken, Benjamin Sisko shuffled forward behind the abrasive and abusing Cardassian lieutenant, who had Sisko and the others in tow on a long rope. Not the usual arrangement, to be sure; there were no handcuffs or strength-sapping cerebroclamps on their heads. But still, the Cardassian sergeants at the gate of the landing zone braced to attention as the unrecognized but thoroughly Cardassian officer passed them by, returning their salutes with nothing but an imperious snort.

The sergeants did not look too closely at the

motley prisoners—*Thank fortune!* thought Sisko; if they had, they would have wondered what two humans, a Klingon, and a *Ferengi* of all people were doing on Sierra-Bravo. But the bored sentries saw only a Cardassian lieutenant dragging behind him four prizes of war, clothed and hooded like many other Natives. *Why should they be alarmed and alert?* thought the captain, *the* Defiant *must already have left orbit—there is no reason to suspect there is anyone here but the Natives . . . if indeed, they truly are native.*

Ahead of Sisko, Quark began to grumble. "Did you have to tie our hands so tight, you sadistic thug?" he snarled.

Cardassian Odo turned his head back. "What makes you think I tied anyone else's hands as tightly as I did yours, Quark?" Sisko couldn't see through Quark's hood, but he was sure the Ferengi was flushing pink with anger.

They were lucky with the clothing. The hoods had come with the scouting backpacks, attached to parkas in case of rain. Chief O'Brien—now directly behind the captain and grumbling quite convincingly—cut the hoods off at the shoulders. Added to the replicated homespun they had worn since first beaming down to the surface, the hoods looked no more bizarre than the costumes of many other Natives, and of course, they hid Klingon, Ferengi, and even human features from prying eyes.

Odo himself had suggested the ruse: he had been

practicing shapeshifting to a Cardassian since *DS9* was *Terok Nor*. His facial features hidden behind a mask, he could pass cursory muster as a "generic Cardassian." So long as they moved fast and the sentries were not particularly alert, there should be no alarm, thought Sisko.

"Are we alone?" he whispered behind him; the column paused while the chief, shielded by the other "prisoners," scanned with his tricorder.

"Besides the two we just passed and the other, there are eleven Drek'la in this structure, and I'm picking up electromagnetic leakage of the frequency used by several models of Cardassian skimmers." O'Brien put away the tricorder and nodded appreciatively to the captain. "You were right, sir; I think it's a vehicle pool."

The structure was one of nine hastily erected buildings ranging from a small Quonset hut with sleeping arrangements for four to a large building emitting a stench that clearly marked it as a Cardassian mess hall. Sisko found the structure that was most centrally located. He couldn't see any vehicles from the angle they viewed, poking their heads over the last rocks of the hilly range against which the split-heads had carried them, but the empty bays he could see looked like loading docks. Captain Sisko made the intuitive leap that they would find skimmers in this building if they found them anywhere.

They left their mounts grazing excitedly on the near side of the hills, chattering among themselves:

evidently, the grass really was bluer on the other side of the desert, or so the herd decided. Ruut and Arrk chomped happily while the females cavorted; within seconds, the entire herd had utterly forgotten the "small-head Idiot" Quark and his own herd . . . *which is just fine with me,* thought Sisko. The split-heads did not exactly go silent.

Creeping down from the hills and cutting around a quarter circle to appear to come from the road, Odo, disguised as the Cardassian lieutenant, led the rest of the away team as prisoners past the sentries, another guard, and now the garage. Sisko looked around in wary satisfaction; the first stage had gone well, and they were in the building without raising alarm. "So we're in," he ventured. "Anybody have a plan now for getting us *out?*"

CHAPTER 13

"WORF, ODO, secure the corridor," said the captain, worrying that at any moment, some Drek'la might take it into his head to check out a skimmer and go cruising. The Klingon and constable parted, each taking position at the closest intersection in each direction. Sisko stood still and quiet in the center, absently stroking his beard—*I desperately need a trim,* he noted—and pondering the undetected removal of a large skimmer from the compound.

"Sir," said Chief O'Brien, interrupting Sisko's thought processes, "wouldn't it be better to leave thievery to a professional?"

"How dare you!" exclaimed Quark, putting on Innocent Look Number Five. "Must I continually be insulted, when I've done every task required of me? Risen above and beyond the call of profit, even!"

O'Brien smirked. "But you instantly knew who I meant, Quark. If the shoe fits, and all that."

Suddenly realizing his vulnerable position, the Ferengi made a sour face and lapsed into awkward silence. He broke it himself after only a few seconds. "Well, actually," he muttered, "I do have a thought. Not through any experience in—in *theft,* but simply because Ferengi businessmen are eternally resourceful and not hampered by useless codes of altruism or chivalry."

"Or honesty," added the chief.

"There's nothing more dangerous than an honest businessman," quoted Quark loftily.

"Rule of Acquisition Number Twenty-Seven," said the captain, startling both disputants. "Now be quiet, Chief, and let the man have his say." Sisko nodded at the Ferengi, who snorted in O'Brien's direction and continued.

"It occurred to me," said Quark, with a bitter glare in the direction of Odo, still shapeshifted into a Cardassian visage, "that the Cardassians would never believe that the—the Natives would have the initiative to steal a skimmer. They've obviously figured out how passive the Natives are about their technology, which is why the Cardassians are doing what they're doing."

"True enough," said the captain; so far, Quark's reasoning was sound.

"So if *a* skimmer, one skimmer, suddenly turned up missing, they might think first to a Drek'la—until they located them all. And then, somebody would remember the *Defiant* and jump to the obvious conclusion."

"That we had managed to beam an away team down before the ship left," said Sisko, seeing where the Ferengi was leading.

"*A* skimmer?" asked O'Brien. "You said if *a* skimmer, one skimmer went missing."

"Exactly!" Quark smiled benignly as if complimenting a child on his first bit of profit earned. "If a whole batch of skimmers disappeared simultaneously, they would first suspect a bizarre computer malfunction."

Sisko grinned broadly, enjoying the image. "If we were to reprogram the routing computers here in the hangar to generate spurious requests for transport and send out all the vehicles, the Cardassians might well think their problem was faulty electronics, not sabotage."

O'Brien seemed none too pleased that Quark had, in fact, thought of a brilliant plan before the chief did, but he had to admit it would be spectacular, if nothing else. Sisko collected Worf and Odo and called them into a huddle. "Worf, you are familiar with Cardassian military-outpost layouts, aren't you?"

"Of course I am," said the Klingon, sounding faintly offended that the captain would even have to ask.

"Being Cardassian, I'm sure they follow a preset and unwavering plan."

"I must admit, the enemy is a model of efficiency and order that the Federation could do well to study."

"Lead us to the main transportation computer, Commander. Chief, you'd better start figuring out exactly what glitch you're going to program while we're en route; we won't have much time between security sweeps."

As was usual in a Cardassian military facility, the corridors were straight, poorly lit by human standards, and scrupulously clean, smelling of ozone and disinfectant from the automated cleaning robots that periodically scuttled past. In case of surveillance, Sisko had Constable Odo lead the way and the rest of the away team act the part of despondent prisoners of war. Worf was directly behind the "Cardassian lieutenant," quietly giving directions.

The Klingon was competent as always, and the crew came to an interior door with markings that read "Transportation Communications Only" in Cardassian. The door was, of course, locked, but the chief began immediately to poke at the touchpad next to it. The door was flimsier than a permanent structure would be, but it was not so weak that they could force their way through . . . everything depended on Chief O'Brien.

Captain Sisko began to count silent seconds as O'Brien worked; there was no way they could explain why a supposed prisoner was being allowed to try to open a locked door! But the captain had barely reached sixteen when the door slid open.

"I bypassed the security protocol," said O'Brien casually. "Don't know why any of us even bother," muttered the chief, half to himself. "Everybody in the whole, bloody quadrant seems able to bypass security codes in half a minute or less."

"It keeps out teenaged joyriders," Sisko couldn't help responding.

The computer room had the best environmental controls of the entire temporary structure, since Cardassian technology (as Chief O'Brien so often reminded the captain) was extraordinarily finicky. The room was maintained at a constant temperature that felt comfortable to Captain Sisko, which meant their hosts would probably have found it chilly. The computers themselves looked far more modern than the systems on *Deep Space Nine*—which made sense, as the Cardassians had built the station many years earlier.

Looking quickly around the room, Sisko saw no permanent sentries, a stroke of good fortune he had anticipated: there was no reason for the invaders to expect to be invaded in turn, and sentries wasted watching an empty room could better serve harrying the population (and grabbing for themselves whatever technology they could lay their hands on). But there might be an occasional roving watchman; best to hurry with their task.

"Chief," said Sisko, gesturing at the nearest console.

"Wait, don't tell me," said O'Brien. "You want me to bypass the security protocols?"

"If you have half a minute."

The internal security must have been more complex than the door entry code; it took Chief O'Brien close to four minutes to find a path around the fire walls. But eventually, he announced he was in and began to enter his virus program. "Six skimmers," he said. "Two of them are the big, ten-person troop transports; the rest are personal cycles." O'Brien continued to work, teasing information out of the console on the fly; Sisko watched in rapt fascination, barely following the blur of coded query, response, and instruction. The man knew his work, no question!

"The years you've spent on the former *Terok Nor* seem to have paid off," said the captain admiringly. O'Brien did not respond.

"Worf," O'Brien asked a few moments later, "do you know where the vehicles are housed?"

"We saw none in the south loading dock," said the commander. "They must all be at the north."

"Good, because we've got three minutes to get to our ride." The chief stood abruptly, absurdly smoothing his rumpled, homespun disguise.

Worf wasted no time. "Back out the door and turn right," he said to Odo, who once more took the actual lead. The Klingon hesitated only twice, but each time, Sisko's heart leapt up his throat. If the three minutes passed, and the computer ordered every vehicle to shove off on mysterious errands before the away team could get to the loading dock, the Federation visitors would be in serious trouble indeed; they might still make it out in the confusion, but the camp would be aroused.

Left, right, through a doorway . . . then there was a footfall ahead of them along a corridor, and the captain grabbed at the nearest door. They hustled inside, Sisko waiting to be last, and only then did he realize he was in the pantry. Ordinarily, he would have waited until the sentry passed, but they had no time: risking the light from torches, Sisko silently pointed to the food stores and indicated every man to stock up. It was a timely serendipity; they were down to their last rationed meal of the food they brought with them on the mission.

No, don't stop! shrieked Sisko inside his skull, as the idiot guard loitered outside the door to the larder. Then an even more worrisome thought occurred: *What if he decides he's hungry and opens the door for an illicit snack?*

But the guard grunted, slapped his belly loudly, and moved on down the corridor. His footsteps had barely faded when the captain threw open the door.

There was no one to see them, and they were down to seconds on the time clock. "No time for stealth," said Sisko. "Run for it! Worf, take point."

"Aye, aye, sir," said the commander, and set off up the replicated-steel hallway at a pace halfway between a jog and a sprint. Odo brought up the rear, still maintaining his Cardassian form—just in case.

They reached the north loading dock. "Damn," said the chief, looking at his tricorder, "we've only got fifteen seconds!"

"Which skimmer did you program for manual control?" demanded Captain Sisko, staring at the parked vehicles.

"Ah, I picked Troop Transport Six," said O'Brien, staring around. "The others are all set to random courses that—"

"No time! Find it!" Even as the captain gave the command, he realized it was unnecessary; there were only two skimmers large enough to be troop transports, and one of them was unmarked . . . probably the personal property of the gul or legate who was in charge of the invasion, a household vehicle rather than military issue. They bolted for the one with military markings, and Chief O'Brien madly pecked at the touchplate.

"Damn it—damn it—*damn* it!" he swore. "Suddenly, I can't bypass a bloody door lock!"

Odo pressed past the captain and yanked O'Brien away from the pad, just as the running lights illuminated and the engines started. Sisko stared at the constable's hand: Odo had turned it into a slim rectangle of plastic with a hook at one end. "Let me try something," mumbled Odo, pushing his shapechanged hand into the door crack, sliding it up, and pulling back. The door opened with a hiss as the troop transport rose slightly from the dock and began to edge out the open end toward the other buildings of the compound.

The away team leapt inside the moving vehicle; again, Sisko insisted on being last . . . and he found himself running full tilt alongside the accelerating skimmer, making a final, desperate leap at the portal. Odo extended his arms like tendrils and caught the captain, reeling him in like a ship in a tractor beam.

The transport picked up speed, and the roar of wind past the open door became deafening; O'Brien, up in the cockpit and swearing like a drunken Klingon, finally found the right command to close it. At last, they could breathe easy; in the rear viewscreen, Sisko watched half a dozen vehicles shoot off in as many directions, followed after a moment by shouting Cardassians on foot, waving their arms and running after the skimmers in a futile attempt to make them turn back.

Quark was staring at Odo. "If I had *known* you would need a SlikPik," grumped the Ferengi, "I would have brought one."

"Oh?" drawled the constable. "And just where would you get such burglar's tools?"

"I use it when I lock myself out of the bar," said Quark austerely.

"Worf," said the captain, cutting off further rejoinder by Constable Odo, "you're Pilot in

Charge. Chief, I want you to get busy with the sensors and find us a central power plant. It's time to put phase two of this mission into effect . . . call it Operation Blackout."

Major Kira Nerys was on duty when the demand came, the first verbal contact they had received from the elusive attackers. Kira stared at the cryptic figures that danced across her threat board; until the computer deciphered them, they had no idea what the aliens were trying to say—or even who they were. Still, even an unintelligible message conveyed information . . . at the least, the aliens were no longer sure of being able to overcome the station before help arrived.

The major slapped her combadge. "Kira to Kai Winn," she said.

"Yes, child?" asked a sleepy voice from the ether; the Kai had just gone to sleep an hour ago.

"They just sent us a message, probably a demand of some sort."

"I shall be right down. Make no response."

Kira shrugged; without knowing what the attackers asked, how could she make any response? It took Kai Winn two minutes to appear in Captain Sisko's "crow's nest," as Chief O'Brien sometimes called it; *probably struggling to put the "serenity" mask back on,* thought the major. During that time, the message from the attackers repeated twice.

Winn said nothing, merely stood behind Kira

and looked at the symbols crawling across the screen. The universal translator struggled, swapping out pieces of the message for jumbles of nonsensical words. The computer took its time, but finally, after an additional six minutes, it had a translation. The words began as "idea sets" in small boxes here and there about the screen, then connector words, refinements, and corrections; abruptly, having gotten the hang of the alien language, the entire message flickered then disappeared, the complete translation replacing it.

> We are the Liberated . . . Survival is the universal right . . . You are overmatched and must surrender . . . You may ultimately keep the enclosed environment but you must pay for your liberty as we paid for ours . . . We require the Portable-Far-Seeing-Anomaly as our price to restore your enclosed environment . . . You must respond within two hours fourteen minutes, thirty-eight point nine one nine one seconds.

Why such a bizarre deadline? thought Kira, momentarily puzzled; she rolled her eyes in exasperation at herself when she realized it was obviously the computer's translation of some "round" number in the aliens' language, probably expressed as vibrations of a helium nucleus or some equally universal unit.

"The *Liberated,*" mused the Kai. "Liberated from what, I wonder?"

"They . . . came from the Gamma Quadrant," suggested Kira.

"Liberated from the Dominion, child?"

Kira shrugged. "They certainly have some Dominionlike technology, but they're significant for what they *don't* have: they haven't beamed anyone out through shields, and they're not using standard Dominion disruptors." Kira winced, eyes dry and painful from staring unblinking at the viewer; she rubbed them. "If they are escaped Dominion subjects who stole vessels, it makes sense that they might not be as well equipped as the Jem'Hadar warships . . . thank the Prophets!"

"If they had come from one of the known Dominion fleets," the Kai pointed out, "they would have come past the Federation-Klingon force in the Gamma Quadrant."

"Which still fits the theory, my Kai: escaped slaves would go out of their way to avoid the Jem'Hadar fleets. So what," she asked, turning to the practical, "what are they asking for? What is this 'Portable-Far-Seeing-Anomaly'?"

"I have somewhat of an idea, my child," said Kai Winn softly, "but I dare not say anything until we know what they *know,* and what they only suspect from distant rumor." She fumbled for her combadge, then spoke sharply: "Computer! Begin recording response to the . . . the Liberated.

"Blessed are you and all others before the Prophets," said Winn. "We are a peaceful people. We too are recently liberated from captors. We must understand further what you mean by the Portable-Far-Seeing-Anomaly. Please clarify. We thank you for recognizing our right to survival, and we shall recognize yours. You may depart in peace. We look forward to better communications, understanding, and trade." The Kai nodded, and the computer responded that the message was recorded. "Translate and send it to the ship," she ordered the computer.

"That was clever," said Kira grudgingly, "turning around their line about survival. The 'enclosed environment' is obviously a reference to *Deep*—to *Emissary's Sanctuary.*"

"So I deduced, child. And I think I know what they want."

The Portable-Far-Seeing-Anomaly? "You're wiser than I," she admitted.

"Of course," said Kai Winn offhandedly. "Nami, while we parley, the Liberated are going to try another assault on the station."

"We shall be ready," said the captain of the strike team running Ops; *a Resistance cell!* realized Kira in amazement; the remnant of a cell that Kai Winn had operated during the Occupation?

"Perhaps," said Winn, so quietly that only Kira may have heard her. She sat calmly, irritatingly, in the chair that still cried for Captain Sisko; Winn rested prim hands on proper knees and smiled serenely at the forward viewer, waiting for the reply from the Liberated. Kira felt like a fifth leg on a *filipis* mount. "Nami, is the *package* ready?"

"Not yet, my Kai," said the tall, grim-faced gunner captain. "It will be brought to your quarters when it's finished."

Winn nodded, understanding the conversation even if Kira hadn't a clue. "Major," said the Kai, startling the executive officer from her reverie, "shouldn't you take personal charge of the militia? That seems a fit task for my second-in-command."

Major Kira brightened; roaming the station under arms would be a welcome distraction from the gears within gears of the Kai's ambassadorial intrigues. At least it was clean, and Kira knew just what to do! "At once, my Kai," she replied, and mounted the turbolift before Winn could change her mind.

The village was a charnal house. Julian Bashir wanted to throw himself to the ground screaming, cover his eyes, and especially block out the stench from several hundred dead bodies left unburied under a hot, white sun . . . *three hundred and forty-four dead bodies, to be precise,* he thought in gory detail. The medical tricorder shook in his hands, but he suppressed all other reactions; he was a doctor, and this was a medical situation. Sort of.

Jadzia had no such rock to cling to; she wrapped her arms around herself and stared at mass homicide, face pale and neck-spots bone white. Gone was the easy banter; three hundred and forty-four massacred innocents shocked even her ancient memory. "They're all dead?" she asked, voice trembling slightly.

"By now, there are no survivors," he answered, professionally reassuring without even thinking about it.

"By *now?* You mean . . . there *were* survivors, but they starved or bled to death?"

Julian didn't answer. Having found no higher life-forms, he searched for genetic scrapings of Cardassians and Drek'la, finding them in abundance.

"Julian. Don't you see what this is? They're slaughtering the Natives all over the planet, just like the Tiffnaki village!" Her voice turned icy. "You forget. I watched this once." She stared so hard at Julian, he actually felt her eyes on his flushed cheeks; he was drawn to look at her even against his will. "'A time to kill,'" she quoted, "'and a time to heal.' It's time to fight back, Julian. For doctors as well as soldiers." He swallowed, recognizing the chime of truth.

Still, Julian Bashir, man of adventure, was still a man of medicine, and it took much, much to turn him into a man of war. "I have fought before," he said guardedly.

Jadzia stared at him with a cold gaze he recognized with a shock as being more of Worf than Dax; he bit his lip painfully, then recalled that she was blood brother to several Klingon warriors of the old school when "she" was a he, Curzon Dax. Jadzia did not see that tie as dissolved, even a death and another life later; there was good reason that Commander Worf accepted her as his equal in matters Klingon.

She spoke almost too softly for him to hear; she sounded reverent, as if she were in a temple instead of an abattoir. "Think of it as triage, Julian. The only way to stop the slaughter is to seize the Cardassians's attention. And I know only one way for sure to do that."

The doctor closed his eyes, but the smell was even more powerful than the sight: the corpses had lain for some time in the sun with no stasis, no refrigeration. *Triage; letting some die that others might live.* It was always the most horrific part of being a doctor, especially a frontier doctor; it was a task he had filled many times, and he still had nightmares about it.

"All right, Jadzia; you win. You want to attack the Cardassians and get them searching for saboteurs instead of slaughtering Natives . . . you're right. I'll do it." He swallowed, feeling a lump where his gorge had risen.

Dax smiled disturbingly and said something in Klingon, which Julian's universal translator implant rendered as, "We shall drink of his blood and sup on his brains." It sounded like a typical Klingon aphorism. "There's a weapon storage on the skimmer," she added. "I already checked. Four fully powered disruptors. We'll head back toward the Tiffnaki village, then track the away team's scent using our tricorders. But the first Cardassian encampment we find . . ." She looked to the bodies at her feet, curling her lip in revulsion.

"Aye, aye, sir," said Bashir coldly, leaving no doubt on whose head the responsibility would lie.

CHAPTER 14

CHIEF MILES EDWARD O'BRIEN shifted his attention between two types of Cardassian sensors, both tuned to detect power broadcasts across the entire electromagnetic spectrum, as well as any subspace transmissions below the communications spectrum. Neither sensor gave very accurate readings; they had already overflown two false alarms, and Worf was beginning to grumble about "incompetence." O'Brien wasn't quite sure whether the Klingon pilot meant *Cardassian* incompetence or O'Brien's.

"Are you certain this time that you have located a power generator?" demanded the commander. "I do not wish to see yet another relay station."

"No, Worf, I'm not certain! I didn't design this

bloody planet, or these piles of rubbish the Cardassians use for sensors."

Worf spoke through clenched teeth, manifestly refusing to look at the chief as he spoke. "Must I remind you that the longer we stay aloft hunting for the generators, the more chance we will be spotted and shot down."

"You don't have to remind me, sir. What do you want me to do, rebuild the bloody things?"

NOW he turns to look at me! "Yes," said the Klingon, "that is an excellent idea."

Sighing in exasperation, Chief O'Brien dropped to hands and knees and pried open the circuit-system cover. The design was a mess, as usual, no better than the spaghetti wiring of *Deep Space Nine*—but no worse, either. Given time, O'Brien decided he could probably rebuild the Cardassian sensor into something closer to the Federation standard.

The question was mooted, however, when a deep voice behind the cockpit pair exclaimed, "There it is, gentlemen. I will stake my command that that is a full power generator." O'Brien looked back over his shoulder at the captain, then turned to see what Sisko was looking at; the chief saw a huge, domed structure lying low to the ground, flat black—not the black of paint or natural stone but the luminous abyss of a powerful force shield.

O'Brien stared, open mouthed; the generator, if that's what it was, was ten times the size of the main Federation shipyards in Earth orbit! "We're not cutting through that," he breathed, watching the shield strength indicator slide off the scale.

Then he brightened. "On the other hand, we may not have to . . . there are two-score power relays surrounding the central plant, and that means there *might* be power conduits connecting them." He pointed to a number of smaller structures, each boasting a monstrous, black antenna, each a microwave "hot point" beaming tight bursts of electromagnetic energy toward distant relays en route to blanketing some portion of Sierra-Bravo.

"Captain," said Worf preemptorally, "where should we put down?"

If Captain Sisko was about to answer, he never got the chance. Every instrument on the control panel lit up like a supernova, and before O'Brien could shout a warning, the skimmer screamed like a terrified child, the metal rending apart under assault from some terror weapon that behaved nothing like a clean disruptor or phaser!

O'Brien felt the impact like a blow to the back of his neck, and he fell from his chair, stunned and dizzy. Everyone else was thrown to the deck, yet somehow Worf managed to keep his seat. The chief's arms still buzzed with the angry bees of severe electrical shock, and he saw Worf's hands shaking violently . . . but the Klingon drew upon reserves deep within his case-hardened DNA to fight through floccillation for control of the ship.

Worf howled like a savage, as if he had forgotten the use of speech—but not how to control a

Cardassian skimmer! The commander shook and jerked spasmotically, and the ship rolled and yawed, dipping in sudden, nauseating drops, but it remained intact and crept ever closer to the ground. *Thank God for lousy Cardassian technology!* prayed the chief: a so-sophisticated *Federation* runabout would probably have splintered into a hundred shards, the delicate electrocolloidal field systems melted into slag by the focused electromagnetic beam that (O'Brien was convinced) had just slugged the skimmer . . . *must've just passed through one of the damned microwave power relays,* he guessed—the analytic portion of his mind still working through the terror at the impending crash.

"Grab—something—solid!" Worf managed to articulate; the chief tried to respond, but the words would not come; he could only moan in frustration and wrap his arms around a cargo net built into the bulkhead. Sick to his stomach, head spinning, he closed his eyes and just wished everything would be over, one way as good as another. Death was preferable to the way he felt at that moment!

The shock of the "landing," if one could use the term for a partially controlled crash, was nearly as bad as the shock that had damaged their skimmer. Worf ploughed a long furrow in the dirt, kicking up twin rooster tails behind the vehicle as it skidded to a long-delayed halt against one of the power relay stations. Exhausted, Worf finally succumbed to the electrocution; he half rose, then fell to the deck, clutching his stomach.

After an indeterminate time interval, someone helped the semiconscious chief to a sitting position, back against one bulkhead. It was Constable Odo, who had pulled himself together quicker than anyone else. O'Brien looked around the cabin, blinking at the terrifically bright light that slowly dimmed as his dilated pupils contracted to their normal diameter. Quark was holding his ears and complaining volubly to no one, since no one was listening; Captain Sisko was sitting quietly, observing without speaking; and Worf was already climbing painfully to unsteady feet. Chief O'Brien was the last to recover speech, but thereafter he recovered quickly.

"Here would be fine for a landing, Worf," said the captain dryly. The Klingon let out an exasperated sigh and shook his head. "Is anybody injured?" asked Sisko.

A small, terrified voice spoke up: "By the—by the Great Accountant . . . *I've lost the will to turn a profit!*" Quark's eyes were nearly as huge as his lobes.

"Well," said Odo, "it seems even the darkest cloud has its latinum lining."

"I'm serious!" wailed the Ferengi; "I must have received a head injury . . . I feel overwhelmed by gratitude merely to be alive—I feel like giving away all my possessions to the nearest beggar in grateful thanksgiving!"

"Feel his head," suggested Worf.

"So our Ferengi felon has converted to a Bajoran

saint," said the constable in disgust. "Do you expect us to believe that, Quark?"

"I don't care what you believe," grumbled the Ferengi, struggling to his feet and massaging his lobes. "I'm seriously injured. I need medical attention."

O'Brien stood, shaking each limb in succession; nothing felt broken. "I think I'm all right," he said. Captain Sisko nodded in a distracted fashion, which annoyed the chief. "If you don't mind," he said stiffly, "I'll pop out and check the damage on the skimmer." Sisko waved without looking round, still intent upon the navigational panels, which were sparking like a Bajoran fireworks show.

O'Brien pressed the recessing door button, and the door ground slowly open, shrieking horribly but still working. He blinked in the brightness, shielding his eyes from the glare off the power relay; wishing he had polarizing lenses, he shaded his eyes and did a fast walk-around. The skimmer was in better shape than he had imagined; the hull could take some repairs, but it looked like it would hold together . . . though a microscan with a tricorder was in order to look for stress fractures invisible to the naked eye. The nose array was snapped off, but Chief O'Brien found it a few meters away; it could be reattached. His biggest fret was the starboard engine, which had a split turbine; the turbine was not strictly necessary for operation, but without it, the engine would overheat. *We'll have to be careful, not take too long a flight;* O'Brien made a mental note to move some of the heat sensors to the broken engine for constant monitoring.

He returned to the cabin. "Overall, it's still flyable on the outside, sir," the chief reported. "Will you let me take a look at the forward panel, if you're all through playing with it?"

"Do you smell something sweet?" asked Quark, sniffing and looking around the cabin.

"The panel is nonoperational," rumbled Worf.

"If you don't mind?" Not waiting for an answer, the chief pushed past the Klingon and stuck his head into the access port. He saw the problem immediately: the control transports had shorted against the fire wall on impact . . . it happened often enough on *Deep Space Nine* after minor shocks from weapons fire or even a hard docking.

Gingerly, he pulled the metallic wires from the metal wall. "You just have to get used to the primitive circuitry," he explained, not sure whether anyone could even hear him. "The Cardassians don't always use fiberoptics . . . sometimes they use copper wiring. There, that should do it," he said, climbing back out from the hood.

Nothing happened; the board remained dark. The stench of ozone filled O'Brien's nostrils. Frowning, he kicked the front panel sharply, and the navlights flickered once, then came back on. "There."

"Impressive," said Sisko, leaning close; Odo and Worf stared at the operational control panel in puzzlement and annoyance, respectively. The chief looked around. "Say, where's Quark got to?"

That woke up the constable, who swiveled his head around like a bird, then darted out the open door. "Miserable little miscreant always disa—!"

"Leave the panel hot," said the captain. "Let's follow Quark and his keeper and see how, exactly, we can get inside this power plant."

Outside, O'Brien squinted against the brightness, turning until he saw the silhouette of Constable Odo. Approaching, the chief saw Odo squatting down, yanking on some large object that appeared bolted or otherwise stuck to the ground. Nearer, he could hear the object bellowing with a Ferengi voice he knew far too well.

"I can *smell* it! I can smell it! Can't you?" Quark had attached himself by hands and feet both to a metal trap in the earth; try as he might, the constable could not wrench him away.

"Odo, Quark, please!" commanded Captain Sisko; Odo stood and shifted away, looking surly, though it could have been the glare in O'Brien's eyes. "Now, Quark," continued Sisko, "what are you *doing* down there?"

Quark turned back to the rest of the team, insane, staring eyes burning like the top of the power relay tower. "There's *LATINUM* here!" he shouted, like a Bajoran enthusiast praying to the Prophets for deliverance from the world. "I can feel it."

"Well," said Odo, "that heartfelt conversion didn't last long."

"Glad to see you're feeling better," said the captain with a straight face. He turned to O'Brien. "Chief, am I mistaken? Or does latinum make a damned good insulator? I mean for a—"

"A power conduit," finished Chief O'Brien, grinning. "Yes, sir. I mean, no sir, you're not wrong. What say we pop the lid and see what our friend has been smelling?"

The lid was a metallic grating, oval, solid, and very, very massive. None of the team could get a grip on it except Constable Odo, who turned his hands into suction cups; but even he couldn't lift it, not even with Worf tugging on one arm and Sisko and O'Brien on the other. They pondered the dilemma; *the damned thing must weigh a couple of tons!* calculated the chief.

Then he rolled his eyes in exasperation at his own stupidity. "Oh, for the love of . . . !" He dug into his pocket and extracted the small handful of toys that he had taken off the Terrors of Tiffnaki at the captain's orders; sifting through, he found the one he wanted and slid the rest back to their pocket. "Allow me," he said, and with a flourish, pointed the antigravity beam at the gigantic manhole. He raised it with ease, placing it gently onto the ground nearby . . . a much more satisfactory conclusion than the last time they had used antigrav to levitate Arrk the split-head.

Quark was first to the pit, folding himself double to stuff his head inside the tunnel. The Ferengi started shouting so excitedly and waving his arms that he toppled over the lip before anyone could grab him. The captain tilted his head at the open hole. "O'Brien," was all he said.

The chief of operations sat on the hole, looked down, and lightly dropped inside. Quark was on his hands and knees, trembling like a young Irish lad peeping through the bedroom window of the colleen next door. The Ferengi spoke slowly and huskily: "The walls—and floor—and ceiling are lined—with *pure latinum."* Quark turned to look back at O'Brien, and his beady, Ferengi eyes were glazed over. "Not gold-pressed latinum. Not latinum plated. Pure—latinum contained in vein-like wires!" Then Quark giggled.

Chief O'Brien unslung his tricorder and swept the long, tubelike corridor. "The power potential is off the scale," he called up to the captain. "If this were an EM field instead of a Pauli potential field, we'd both be fried to a crisp." He shut off the tricorder, nervous that the probing sensor beam might accidentally collapse a state vector and bring the potential field into incinerating reality. "I'd say we found what we were looking for, sir."

Captain Sisko followed his two team members, then Constable Odo (unhappy at Quark being out of sight for even a moment), finally Worf bringing up rear guard. Everyone but the Ferengi had to crouch in the low conduit; Worf worked himself around so he was facing backwards, away from the main power plant, where the conduit extended an additional fifty meters, for "kinetic-resonance echoing," according to O'Brien—*whatever the hell THAT is!* Thc Klingon would have to walk backward to keep up with them, but it allowed him to cover their exit.

This whole thing is spooky, thought the captain as they scrunched along the conduit toward the heart of a reactor big enough, according to O'Brien's tricorder, to power six stations the size of *Deep Space Nine* . . . or *Emissary's Sanctuary,* as it was now, and probably would remain being, called. The cold echoes of boot steps on the latinum flooring did indeed resonate up and down the power conduit, rattling Sisko's skull and shaking loose stray thoughts and random memories: he felt a terrible pang of unexpected regret leaving the station behind; if—when!—the *Defiant* returned and the crew drove away the Cardassians from Sierra-Bravo, Benjamin Sisko would be taken back not to the station that had been his home for five years, but to a new command, a new assignment. *Probably a ship tour,* he thought, *since the station counts as an out-of-sequence shore tour.*

But that was only speculation; for all the captain knew, he could end up chief administrator of another starbase, or teaching classes at the Academy, or even serving four years in the hallowed halls of Starfleet Command, trailing after some old admiral, wiping the man's chin when he drooled. In the grand scheme of Starfleet, a low-seniority captain was not a very high rank at all. No one except Sisko's detailer would even ask his preference, and the "needs of the service" would take precedence anyway. *As they did five years ago, after Jennifer died,* he recalled; the only thing he had wanted after that Borg attack was to resign and spend the rest of his life in morbid self-pity.

Trouble—Quark looked almost mesmerized by all the pure latinum surrounding him . . . though on Sierra-Bravo, latinum was as commonplace as iron on Earth. But the greedy, little Ferengi was trembling like a fevered patient, plucking at the bulkheads, the overhead, a man caught in a dream that was rapidly turning nightmarish: there was *nothing* Quark could do! He had to close his eyes to profit like no Ferengi had ever seen and forget all about Sierra-Bravo. Whatever he saw, whether raw resources or prime technology, belonged to the Natives . . . not to the Cardassians, the Federation, or to Quark.

But every membrane in his lobes must have been screaming at him to plot, scheme, do anything to get his hands on that profit! Quark could be near to breaking; more than religion, the Ferengi pursuit of profit was close to a biological compulsion. Quark fought it with as much agony as Odo fighting to remain solid day after day: *sooner or later,* realized

Sisko, *he'll break again* . . . as he had twice before on the mission.

And Odo isn't helping, thought the captain, frowning; the constable was being particularly obtuse, riding Quark harder, if anything, than he did back on the station. Perhaps a candid talk was in order, but Captain Sisko did not look forward to that duty. The shapeshifter could be remarkably touchy and adamant in his administration of "justice."

Sisko banged his head, only then noticing that the conduit was narrowing as they approached the reactor. "Worf, duck lower," he called back over his shoulder. The only light was the sharp, bluish glow from Quark's chemical glowtubes and the shaky beams from the hand torches carried by the rest of the team. Sisko felt a sudden, horrible sensation of claustrophobia; the walls were merely narrowing, but his mind insisted they were squeezing tight as he watched them! A clutching compulsion to turn around and claw madly back the way he had come swept through the captain; only the even stronger fear of humiliation and loss of command respect stopped him . . . that and the fact that he probably couldn't turn around now even if he wanted; the conduit was too narrow.

The feeling subsided but didn't abate entirely. Captain Sisko gave no outward sign; if command had taught him one great lesson, it was that life imitates artifice: pretend courage and confidence, and soon you feel them for real. Past Quark and

O'Brien, Sisko saw a grating that incorporated both latinum mesh and some sort of energy cobweb. "It's behind that," said the chief, nodding at the grate.

"And if we opened a hole in that mesh?"

"It would be like opening up a window into the core of a star," was the crisp and very visual reply.

CHAPTER 15

SISKO STARED for a long moment. One by one, though no command was given, the teammates turned off their lights, leaving only the cobalt blue of Quark's chemical light and the yellow glow of the latinum energy mesh. Bizarre, curved lines of bright light played across the faces of the away team as Sisko looked at each one in turn: ionized plasma trails from subatomic particles fleeing the horrific maelstrom of creation-destruction within the power generator, Shiva and Krishna waltzing to quantum pipes. "If we blew a sudden hole," he mused, "I wonder whether they'd see the flare all the way to the Cardassian camp?"

"I'd say," responded O'Brien, "it would light up

the sky, for certain. A disruptor set to overload, do you think?"

Sisko stared at the grating, visualizing what it held back on the other side. "Doubtful. A disruptor overload would be a drop in the proverbial bucket."

"You're probably right, sir." O'Brien closed his eyes, thinking out loud. "The grating must convert actual energy to quantum potential; no physical cable or energy field could transport that much energy without melting. Then the relays convert it back to broadcast power, stepping it down enough that all those pretty toys can use it."

"And were does all this analysis get us, Chief?"

O'Brien shrugged, still at a loss.

Quark softly cleared his throat; when the captain and operations chief fell silent to look at the green-tinted Ferengi, he looked almost embarrassed. "I, ah, notice there's an access hatch in the center of the latinum grating."

"It can't be opened while the reactor is hot," explained O'Brien. "It was used when the reactor was designed—probably seven million years ago, assuming the planet was powered up when the buildings were built, if Commander Dax got it right."

"Why can't we open it?" Quark persisted.

"Because it's designed that way!" snapped the chief. "There's no reason to open it then . . . unless you're planning to blow it up." He looked at Captain Sisko.

"That is a problem," admitted Sisko. "Ideally, we don't want to destroy it, just shut it down for a while."

"Well, if we blow this reactor the power surge will trip the equivalent of circuit breakers throughout the planetary grid. We'd have to turn the power back on manually, but that's simple enough. Even the Natives could do it."

"If you two are through interrupting," said Quark, "I do have an idea."

Behind them, Odo snorted. "If Quark wants to contribute an idea, I'd recommend the rest of us sit on him until the feeling passes."

"I'll ignore the comments from the small-head seats. Are you interested in blowing this reactor or not?"

Sisko considered. "Well, let's hear your idea at least," he reluctantly decreed.

Quark grinned, as if closing a deal to bankrupt an enemy, and rubbed his hands gleefully; he appeared to be enjoying his new role as saboteur. His face looked almost demonic in the hellish, green glow from his chemical light. "They designed this panel to resist all the force and pressure on the other side. So it seems to me," he drawled, "that exerting a tremendous force on *this* side might blow the hatch inward."

"We've already thought about a disruptor on overload, Quark," said the captain, wondering what the Ferengi was driving at. "It wouldn't be enough force."

"No, probably not." Quark showed his needle-sharp, uneven, snaggly teeth. "But how about the force beam projector? It was powerful enough to flatten a kilometer of swamp. If we braced it at the back of the tunnel there, pointing toward the hatch—"

O'Brien interrupted derisively. "And are you volunteering to stay here and operate it while the reactor blows?"

"Captain Sisko, I'm sure the chief here can rig up a remote control to operate the thumbslide."

Odo weighed in: "I hate to admit it, but this is basically an exercise in safecracking. Our felonious team member is in his element; he might have something here."

Sisko thought for a long moment; he couldn't delude himself about the enormity of what he contemplated. But he had time; it would take O'Brien an hour or more to rig the remote control, even with Quark's help. *Especially with Quark's interfering help,* thought the captain gratefully. "Chief, begin to construct the trigger; Quark, it's your idea . . . be the chief's assistant."

"But Captain!" protested both simultaneously; each paused and glared suspiciously at the other.

"Go, both of you. I must meditate for a while. Odo, Commander, come with me." Sisko began to back away from the pair up front; looking back over his shoulder, he saw that Odo had contrived to turn around—easier when one is a shapeshifter!—leaving the captain as the only person creeping backward toward the shaft leading up. There, the mouth widened, and Sisko was able to squirm around in the cramped, tomb-smelling tunnel. In the light from the open hole above them, they once again turned off their hand torches.

The sun was sinking, and the giddy, copper glow painted all three an unpleasant, sickly yellow. Odo and Worf waited patiently for the captain to begin.

"What we contemplate," commenced Sisko, "is nothing short of a complete abandonment of the Prime Directive."

"Fighting the Cardassians is perfectly proper," countered Worf. "They don't belong here either."

"But now we're talking about *taking down* the main power reactors for the entire planet!" Odo said.

Sisko held up his hand, and both men fell silent, recognizing that the captain would make the decision. There would be no vote; Benjamin Sisko wanted to hear both arguments framed, but he was the only judge. He, alone, would bear responsibility before a general court-martial, if it came to that; in a survival situation such as this, Starfleet would agree that the only course for his subordinates was to obey orders without demur.

A survival situation . . . A tiny candle flame of an idea flickered in Sisko's mind; he closed his eyes, tried to think of nothing, allowing it to catch and burn bright enough to be seen and felt. *When there is no moral option,* he thought, *then there is no truly immoral choice.* The spirit of the Prime Directive would be violated just as surely by doing nothing and allowing the Cardassians to take over; *may as well be hanged for a cow as a sheep,* thought the captain with a sardonic smile. And James Kirk had faced this choice many times in his career, and had done what was necessary.

"We will continue and destroy the reactor," said Sisko. Odo said nothing; he looked as though he had expected the decision would go against his position.

"I will stand and fight with you before the admiralty," pledged Worf without a hint of amusement.

"I'm sure they'll be duly impressed, Commander." The captain allowed no trace of sarcasm to taint his own words. "But perhaps it will be better, when it comes to that, if you let me do my own talking."

When Chief O'Brien had done with the remote switch—*and a fine job it is, too,* he thought to himself—he backed up until he reached the shaft of light, turned around, and squeezed past the captain to the opposite end of the tunnel. There, O'Brien wedged the force beam projector into a shallow groove that would hold it steady. He turned it on, to the lowest setting. "Quark!" he called, "get back down the tunnel and plant yourself directly in front of the hatch."

"What? Why?" The Ferengi sounded nervous . . . as well he might, considering what maelstrom was behind the mesh wall.

"Just do it! I need to align this thing, or we won't get anything but a dented wall."

"But why do I have to . . ." Quark's voice trailed off as light suddenly dawned in his devious, Ferengi brain. "You want to align it on *me?* You're insane! I won't do it!"

"It's perfectly safe, Quark; it's on the lowest setting. It's not going to blow the door prematurely."

"I'm not standing next to that hatch while you point that thing at it!"

O'Brien made the obvious point. "You really think you'd be any less dead if you stay where you are, and the hatch blows?"

Quark scowled, considering the violence of the expected explosion. "I think I'll take a stroll topside, stretch my legs a bit."

Odo had his own observation: "You might have a hard time getting past me, Quark, and if you did, you'd only have to get past Commander Worf, as well. Now why don't you do what you're told, for once in your life?"

Sullenly, Quark hunched low and began to wriggle down the tunnel, grumbling every step of the way. The Ferengi reached the hatch; he turned and sat gingerly. He looked pale and greenish, but it might have been from the chemical glowtube he still carried, which was starting to dim as the reaction died down.

"Tell me when you feel a force right on your chest," said the chief, turning the force beam projector agonizingly slowly. It took a solid ten minutes to get it set exactly where Chief O'Brien wanted it: directly over the keyhole latch, the weakest spot on the hatch. "I'm giving us fifteen minutes," said O'Brien clearly.

He set the timer to nine hundred seconds and pressed the arm switch, then the activate-countdown thumb pad. He watched it count down to 899, 898, and 897, then rose and suggested, "Let's get the hell out of here, if you don't mind."

Worf was nearest the ladder, and he climbed swiftly but without apparent haste. Odo went next, then Quark.

Captain Sisko had stepped to the ladder to shout at Worf, so O'Brien pushed up behind him; the chief had won the honor of being last man out. Sisko scurried up the ladder, still too slow for the frantic Chief O'Brien. *Fifteen minutes! Why not a half hour, or two hours?*

Odo spun his head around backward disconcertingly. "Why did you set the timer for only fifteen minutes?" demanded the constable, eerily echoing O'Brien's own thoughts.

They bolted to the skimmer, where Worf yanked the door open so hard that O'Brien was momentarily worried the commander would rip it off its hinges. They piled in like a slapstick holoplay. The chief tried to push to the front to fire up the engines, but first Quark, then Odo, then Sisko himself got in the way. By the time O'Brien reached the front panel, he was swearing like a drunken Academy scrub on first liberty.

The navigation and engine-start panel, which they had left hot, was off again. His running commentary of oaths dissolving into half-formulated slurs against Cardassians, O'Brien kicked it again; this time, there was no effect. A second, harder kick also failed to shake loose whatever short circuit had killed the power.

"Perhaps I should try," said Worf with barely concealed animosity.

"No, no!" shouted O'Brien, holding up his hands; the Klingon was still brooding about getting stuck and almost killing everyone. *He'd probably kick a ragged hole right through the forward hull!*

A tiny shape pushed up beside the chief, ducking under O'Brien's groping arms like an annoying child. "Allow me, Chief," said Quark. He was probably trying to be soothing, but his Ferengi sarcasm dribbled through, and O'Brien felt a momentary urge to give Quark's gigantic, pink, hairless skull a left hook that would send the Ferengi reeling into an already furious Worf. The chief mastered his impulse.

"Quark! Get out of there! What the hell do you know about Cardassian engineering or—"

The navigation lights lit up all at once, the power-start switch blinking temptingly. Chief O'Brien fell silent, feeling his face flush with humiliation.

"Nothing," said Quark, "but I *do* know somewhat about Cardassian security systems. They must have unscrambled the computer back at the depot and sent a general recall order to all the skimmers we stole." The Ferengi pulled a piece of equipment from under the hood of the console, where he'd been fiddling, and dropped it into O'Brien's outstretched hand; it was a logic circuit with a receiver attached . . . the chief himself made use of the same devices on the station to manipulate control systems directly on the numerous occasions when the station's Cardassian autonomic computer would go off-line. "Since we had the parking brake set, the skimmer shut off instead."

"Can we get started now, Chief O'Brien?" snapped Worf; he sounded somewhat mollified, now that Quark had taken the focus off of the Klingon. Irked and chagrined, O'Brien tapped rapidly on the console, initiating the electron flow and the positronic counterflow, adjusting the contour map, and finally starting the engines. The repairs they needed could certainly wait until they got away from Ground Zero.

"It's all yours, sir," he said to Worf. Without a word, the Klingon boosted the power to maximum and lifted the shaky, hard-to-control skimmer a few meters off the ground and started it moving—slowly at first, so that O'Brien writhed in his chair, looking back over his shoulder as if his eyes could bore through the rear hull and watch the power plant (though it would be a terrible idea even if it were possible; anybody watching the plant with naked eyes from nearby when it exploded would be blinded, perhaps permanently).

Now Odo crowded the nose of the skimmer, leaving only the captain back in the troop seats. "Commander, can't you get this thing any higher?" demanded the constable.

"It is better to stay low," said Worf. "The blast will be directed primarily upward. Now please return to your seats, both of you! I am tired of having to compensate for your unbalanced weights in the hand controls." Reluctantly, they slithered away back to rejoin Captain Sisko.

"Better strap yourselves in," warned O'Brien, glancing at his chronometer; we've got about twenty seconds before all hell busts loose." He reached across and buckled in the Klingon pilot, who needed both hands on the stick and collective; Worf did not object. O'Brien barely had time to slip into his own harness when every electronic instrument on the console flashed red, then dropped to zero.

At the same time, the landscape forward of the skimmer flared bright white, a searchlight on hard-packed snow. The chief shut his eyes tight, and still the light hurt; as he blinked them open painfully, he saw the afterimage of the veins in his own eyelids as ghostly, pulsating lines, rivers of phantom blood. Tears leaked down his cheeks, and he tried to blink his vision back.

The shock wave struck almost twelve seconds later; O'Brien estimated that they had managed to make about four kilometers from Ground Zero. Judging from the force of the wave at that distance, if they had been any closer, they would have made a smoking crater in the dirt.

The skimmer skewed fiercely, the stern yawing to the left nearly ninety degrees and sinking. Worf had been right; the majority of the shock wave was propelled upward, missing the skimmer entirely. A second later, just as Worf got the ship back under control, they were struck from below by another invisible fist as the wave reflected off the ground; this one was not so severe. The sealed airlocks kept some of the noise out, but the low vibrations shook right through the hull and broadcast a low rumbling inside that was loud enough to make O'Brien shout in pain and clap his hands over his ears.

Then the main shock was over; the electronics rebooted after the electromagnetic pulse, and the rear viewer showed an enormous mushroom cloud rising above the reactor explosion, as, of course, happened in every high-temperature detonation—chemical, thermonuclear, or matter-antimatter.

The ringing in O'Brien's ears quieted, and he thought he heard his name called. Unbuckling shakily, he returned to the central cabin. Quark was unconscious, curled in a fetal position with his arms wrapped around his lobes; Odo was caught unguarded, staring with concern at the man he would never in a thousand years call his friend . . .

but who was doubtless his closest companion on the station.

The captain sat unperturbed on one of the seats, his legs crossed, the portrait of composure. "Chief O'Brien," he began.

"Sir?"

"Next time, let's give ourselves a good thirty minutes—relax a little."

"Aye, aye, sir," said the chief, not entirely displeased. All in all, it had been a pretty full day, as such things went.

CHAPTER 16

FOUR HOURS INTO Major Kira Nerys's tour as commander of the militia, the doors of Hell opened wide, and the False Prophet of Hateful Lies burst through. The enemy had not been idle; while Kira and Kai Winn waited, watched, slept, the escaped captives (if that's what they truly were!) slithered across the abyss between their ships and the station. They used no boarding craft or shuttles or rockets; they jumped across, by ones and twos, softly touching the skin of *Emissary's Sanctuary* and sticking fast with some adhesive or suction tool. Their ships went undetected, their cloaking devices far advanced over the Federation's. The individual invaders were each too small to trigger the station's sensors. Before the first alarm sounded, there were more than a hundred and fifty soldiers crawling across the outer hull!

Steering well clear of the airlock doors, the unsuspected assassins used handheld cutting torches to burn holes through the skin large enough for them to wiggle through in full battle array. The first inkling Kira had was a hastily shouted warning over the com-link, severed before the militiaman could even shout his location.

"Computer!" demanded Kira. "Where did that last transmission come from?"

"Level nineteen, sector thirty-eight," responded the cheerful, dumb-as-dirt contralto.

"Damn it, we're scattered on those lower levels." Closing her eyes to think better, the major tapped her combadge again and summoned three companies to the breakthrough, but before they could reach the right level, beetle-armored invaders were bursting through the hull all over the station.

She ran to her own nearest break and found herself in an instant gun battle with black, featureless aliens shooting a rapid-fire energy pulse weapon that carved through bulkheads like a hot knife through frozen yogurt. She lost Willi and Fienda in the first volley and nearly lost the left side of her face as a bolt cut through the corner of the Klingon restaurant when she peeked around.

"Fall back! Fall back!" The command wasn't quick enough, and her friend Gerti, who was a Dabo girl before Kai Winn took control, took a shot to her stomach; the girl crumbled into a still, white form, clearly dead before her face struck the deck.

The militia retreated, firing back over their shoulders; a lucky shot from Kira took one of the invaders in his leg, bringing him down, but there were no other casualties on the aggressor's side. Their armor was good enough to require a direct and sustained phaser blast to do any damage.

Four hours and twenty-three minutes into Kira's tour, she was a commander without a command, her militia army wracked and scattered, casualties high, walls and shielding chewed like a dog bone. The major was shell-shocked, ordering her steadily diminishing forces in a leaden voice, trying to turn a tide that relentlessly filled the station: the invaders were still swarming across the gap between their undetectable ships and the ruptured *Emissary's Sanctuary*. Ten more minutes of retreat, and Kira was desperate enough to call Winn and beg the Kai to get reinforcements from Bajor.

"What could they do, child?" asked Kai Winn, serene as always. In Kira's present state of mind, the major wanted to reach through the com-link and throttle the old . . . the venerable, middle-aged Kai. Instead, she sagged against the corridor wall outside the hydroponics lab and breathed deeply.

"They could distract the invaders while we—while we—"

"While we launch more futile attacks that stand no greater chance of success than we've had so far?"

Kira closed her eyes, exhaustion wrapping her like a burial shroud. "My Kai, we must do something. We stand to lose the station if we don't!"

"Nerys, what makes you think sitting quietly is doing *nothing?"* While Kira pondered the seemingly nonsensical reply, Kai Winn added a peremptory order disbanding the militia and recalling the major to Ops, relieving her of an impossible command. Kira felt the burning shame of failure, despite knowing there was nothing anybody could have done. *Sometimes the battle is over before it begins,* sighed Shakar once, during the Resistance, when the cell had to abandon a perfect cave to the superior intel and lightning strike of the Cardassians. It made no difference: loss and failure burned her cheeks as they had back when she was a young girl testing herself for the first time.

Wisdom; I pray for the wisdom to see that loss is as inevitable as gain, if you fight long enough. The last weren't the words of Shakar or any other Resistance leader; the quotation came from the first services Kai Winn led as Kai. *The Emissary knows,* Kira thought; Captain Sisko had gleefully told her once of a baseball pitcher who held the all-time record for strike outs . . . and at the very same time, the all-time record for walks, for games won, and for games lost! Not surprisingly, she also held the record for most number of games pitched, the real pillar that underlaid all Katsio Bando's other baseball records.

"I am on my way," said Kira, striving to sound

as calm and contained as her new commander; she achieved only the sound of weariness and regret. Sharply, Kira ordered her few remaining militia members to disperse and hide their weapons, a drill every Bajoran above a certain age knew all too well. The station was already lost; no sense losing all their lives into the bargain. The only hope now for Bajor was that the invaders would make good their offer to allow the station personnel to live.

Kira had her own, private hope, however. Much as it would horrify the Kai, Major Kira still held out hopes that the mighty Federation would indulgently liberate the station, even if it meant another ten years before Bajor could again petition for sovereignty. The wormhole, where the Prophets dwelt, was far more important than the pride of Bajor—or so Kira told herself convincingly.

She kept her own phaser rifle, for her uniform already identified her as military, and ran with her two personal bodyguards back to the turbolift. The shaft was billowing smoke, and the lift was nowhere to be seen; they would have to climb many levels on the ladderways, a prospect Kira viewed with resignation.

As her last task, the erstwhile commander of the militia forces decided to speak with the four bombardment shelters scattered on the Quark's Place side of the Promenade; her lieutenant, Maranu Vann, would be doing the same on the other side.

She climbed up to the ninth level, rifle slung over her shoulder. Kira and her guards crept around the rim of the Promenade, scanning for invaders. They were swarming all over the station, their biological peculiarities easy to track, but they had largely abandoned the shattered Promenade with its broken shops and deserted walkway and catwalks. Kira slipped around the perimeter until she came to the first sealed vault.

Then the major, slight as a will o'-the-wisp, slung the rifle back over her shoulder and strode through a security door toward the next shelter on her list. "At least, thank the Prophets, the captain and away team are safe and away from here." Nobody heard her grumble; nobody was meant to.

The demolition squad had got it down to a science. Chief O'Brien had buried most of his qualms; so long as he had a great chain of commissioned officers up top, he didn't have to worry about covering the bottom. But he couldn't quite extinguish the moral reservations: *after all, we're basically throwing these Natives back into the Stone Age!*

All in a "good cause," as Quark kept saying. The Ferengi was the only team member who seemed completely at ease with what they were doing, nuking every power plant on the planet. When O'Brien planted the third modified force beam projector and watched the third generator detonate with an earth-shattering convulsion, he realized his hands were shaking so hard he almost couldn't operate the navigational controls.

He felt nauseated. *No, it's not nausea . . . it's a physical PAIN in my gut, like a big fist punched me in the solar plexus.* Worf was tense at the stick; years on the *Enterprise* with the Klingon gave O'Brien a read. And Sisko had said nothing for several hours, just absently stroked his beard and stared at the horizon.

"Do you need me for anything?" asked Odo. Without waiting longer than two seconds for an answer, he liquified and poured himself up and over the lip of a luggage rack.

"Well, Chief," said the ever smarmy Quark, "looks like it's just you and me. Have I ever told you about the time I played Tongo with Dax?" O'Brien tuned out the Ferengi as he droned on.

At least, thank God, Keiko's warm and safe back on Bajor, he thought; *they're not living through this hell!*

Thirty minutes later, Captain Sisko abruptly spoke, causing O'Brien to jump in his chair. "Commander Worf, set a course for the Tiffnaki village. I think it's about time we see how our commandos and their comrades are taking the sudden change in lifestyle."

CHAPTER 17

THE STATELY Cardassian-Drek'la convoy crawled across the desert. *Cardassians move swiftly from Point A to Point B,* thought Commander Jadzia Dax; *they don't dawdle without a reason.* In this case, she decided, they were out hunting . . . not hunting Natives; they wouldn't consider the defenseless, dazed Natives worth being pursued as game. More likely, she decided, the Cardassian column was out hunting the local cross between a horse and an *ocant,* which Julian had dubbed "cleft-heads" for the deep groove running down their faces from crown to nose.

Observing the captured cleft-heads, Dax realized, to her shock, that they were semiintelligent; it was an open question whether they could talk, but it seemed likely. Evidently, the Cardassians had figured out that much as well: they had recently gone on several hunts in as many days, observed by herself and Julian Bashir. But so far, there had been no good opportunity for an ambush.

"Julian," she asked, speaking softly even though the column was more than a kilometer away, down in the desert valley below the hills where the Federation scouts crouched, "how many species on this planet do you suppose are intelligent?"

"Define intelligent," countered the good doctor. "What about the blue, six-legged lizards?"

Dax shuddered at the memory: a dozen of the reptilian beasts, almost a meter long each, were arrayed in a semicircle around a larger version, who was making a number of faint squeaks by expanding his throat and expelling air through gill-like slits on the back of his throat. It was too far away for the universal translators to make out any words—if there were any words—but the lizard audience dipped their heads in unison, as if responding to a lecture, or worse, an aria.

"Jadzia," said Bashir, "we may have stumbled onto a planet where intelligence evolved early on, and virtually every creature advanced enough to be mobile developed some."

"Alternatively," she ventured, "whoever put the Natives and the tech here also liked to play gruesome games with genetic engineering." Julian grunted, acknowledging the possibility. "In any case, changing the subject, I believe we've finally got a winner in the Target Lottery. All the signs are good: no two-headed snakes or fiery clouds on the horizon."

"Aye, aye, ma'am." Somehow, the tragic figure managed to convey his deep regret and sorrowful acceptance of the cruel necessities in a mere three words. Bashir raised his disruptor rifle; Dax sited along hers, picking out the lead skimmer full of soldiers.

"I've got the front; you take the second vehicle. The first shot has to be simultaneous, Julian, or they'll dive into cover; ready?"

"In my sites."

"Three, two, one, fire." She depressed the trigger button, and nothing happened. "Damn it!" she snarled, clicking off the safety and fingering the button again. Julian's disruptor shot first, of course, but Dax followed on quickly enough that the lead Cardassians weren't even aware yet that their comrades had been attacked.

Bashir and Dax were too far away to hear any immediate screams or explosions as the beams ignited power cells on the skimmers. About three seconds later, when the sound waves traversed the thousand meters from target to attacker, the Federation snipers heard the first, faint noise from the assault: a loud boom, followed by faint cries of agony from those singed but not killed outright by the beams.

They returned fire, of course; their shots swept across the rock escarpment, but it was no difficulty for Dax and Bashir to duck back. The invaders had no chance: they couldn't even see where the ambush came from, and with every shot, the Federation insurgents whittled away at the Cardassian numbers.

Dax heard a steady beep. "We're being scanned," she said offhandedly.

Finally, a few soldiers got smart and tried to take cover behind the skimmers, but it was too little, and far too late: Dax and Bashir picked all but one of them off before they made cover, and the last lost his composure and stood in plain view for a last-chance shot . . . *like he's committing suicide,* thought Dax; *or better, perhaps,* hara-kiri.

The smoke from the burning skimmers drifted skyward, bending to the right in the close breeze. The titanium frames finally caught fire, which meant there would be nothing left of the vehicles by the time the flames burned out, for virtually nothing could stop the incredibly exothermic burning of titanium.

As Julian Bashir and Jadzia Dax approached, scanning the horizon with Dax's tricorder to watch for the enemy (who surely would come to investigate the battle), the commander thought she saw something moving. Squinting, she caught sight of a lone figure crawling away from the wreckage, behind which he had been hiding.

It took the two away team members twenty-five minutes to reach the carnage, but in that time, the lone survivor hadn't gotten very far. He lay sprawled on the sandy, desert floor, his mouth stuffed with a gul's ransom of rare minerals, coughing up smoke and blood.

Dax stood over the man, who was dressed as a high-ranking officer, though she couldn't see his rank so long as he lay face down. She slowly raised her disruptor, her thumb on the trigger button. The Cardassian stiffened, evidently feeling her behind him, feeling the finger of death brush his heart.

Instinctively, Dax pulled her scarf up to cover her mouth and nose and saw Julian do the same. Their hoods already obscured the rest of their faces, except for their eyes, and they were dressed in clothing that could well be Native styles. They held disruptors obviously taken from other Cardassians . . . there was nothing to tell the man—a gul, Dax noted—that they were anything but local resistance fighters.

"Don't—kill—me," he said, wheezing, his lungs bruised by breathing the smoke from the burning skimmers. "Worth money . . . worth—trade."

Dax said nothing in response, and Bashir followed her lead; there was no telling what the Cardassian equivalent of the universal-translator implant would tell him about the language it was translating; if it alerted him they were speaking Federation standard, they would lose the advantage that their presence was still unsuspected.

But he knew what they waited for; beaten and

sick, he offered what little he had left: his name. "Gul," he coughed; "Gul . . . Ragat. Ragat, the—the Banished."

The name meant nothing to Jadzia Dax, and she could think of no reason why it should.

Kira climbed through the emergency trap into Ops, followed by her two lieutenants . . . now little more than personal bodyguards. Captain Virgat Maav and second Lieutenant Arno—Kira never knew the woman's given name—took station on either side of the turbolift shaft. The Kai's defense cell had already sealed the shaft by phaser-welding hull-material grillwork across it; the barrier would probably last two seconds after the beetle aliens turned their concentrated fire upon it, Kira decided. But it was a nice gesture.

"All right, I'm here, my Kai," she said. Kai Winn stood in front of the Ops consoles staring at the forward viewer, which showed only the shadowy outlines of invader ships when they passed between the station and some known constellation. *Even the ships look like armored insects,* thought Kira morbidly; she decided she had developed a morbid coleopterophobia lately.

Kai Winn said nothing; she gazed at the viewer, and not coincidentally, at the wormhole . . . though nothing was to be seen unless a ship would come through. Kira shifted uncomfortably from one to the other foot, wishing she were anywhere but where she was, not for fear, but for embarrassment; the major couldn't decide whether she was shamed by the Kai, humiliated by the situation, or condemned by her own conscience. She had failed, the station fallen, her command obliterated, the dream of Bajoran independence torn away like the wings off a sparklefly.

No one could have done better, she tried to tell herself. Her guilt answered, *but none could do any worse.*

"Kai Winn, what do we do now?"

Kira jumped; for a moment, she thought she, herself, had asked the unaskable. But it was Captain Maav, a middle-aged middle manager who looked like what he had been before the turnover: an architect designing shrines and temples, the occasional secular public building. Before that, she recalled, he was a captain in the Freedom Brigade Reserves—hence the rank. And before that, Kira vaguely recalled meeting him at an all-cells gathering during the Resistance, a face partially obscured in the crowd who was introduced (no names, of course) as something-or-other critical to some cell she'd never heard of before.

Captain Maav was not the man to sit stolidly doing his job and awaiting orders. He ran his own firm. He was used to giving orders and couldn't quite break the habit of bluntness even when speaking to the Kai.

She turned and smiled sweetly at his question; Kira felt a twinge of—Prophets, could it be *jealousy?*—that the Kai had responded instantly to

Virgat Maav but not at all to Kira Nerys. "Do? Is there anything else to do?" Kai Winn squared her shoulders and cleared her throat. "Computer, please broadcast this message station-wide."

At first, Kira's eyes widened. *Please? She's asking the computer's pardon?* Then an inkling of what the Kai must be about to say penetrated, and Major Kira felt tiny insects tumble inside her stomach. She shivered, feeling her knees weaken. *I know what she's going to say!* screamed Kira's intuition. A moment of crystal precognition, premonitory trembling at what was to come momentarily.

"Children of the Prophets," began the Kai reasonably enough, "followers of the Word, free citizens of Bajor"—

Maybe she's going to exort us to fight to the last man! wished Kira, but she could not wish away what she already knew.

—"and visitors from beyond the realm of the Prophets, what you must call the wormhole. I bid you peace, welcome, and the blessings of the Prophets."

Bile erupted up Kira's throat, singeing her esophagus. Her forehead began to drip. She felt a flicker of dizziness.

"I sorrow that we have met in such inauspicious and unpleasant circumstances. But the meeting need not be disastrous, nor catastrophic. There need be no more shedding of blood or loss of life."

Decades of Resistance . . . only to sink to this!

"We take you at your word that you have no

designs upon the inhabitants of *Emissary's Sanctuary.* We grieve for your captive status, so recently alleviated. We share that bond; we, too, have recently purchased our own freedom from oppression with our blood, our sweat, and our faith."

Kira could no longer stand. She fell heavily into the seat usually occupied by the sensor-intercept officer, a position the Kai had decided she didn't need. *Not that it would have made any difference with these invaders,* thought Kira; their cloaking devices were too good. The major slumped in her seat, feeling faint. None of the other warriors of the Kai's inner circle could look at their leader. Even the Kai's personal defense cell studied their consoles as if they would find the secret of the Final Prophecies written there, plain for all to see.

"We have no wish," continued the Kai, unperturbed, "to prolong this mistaken struggle. Clearly, we have both of us failed to communicate with each other. We have no enemies in this quadrant, and we are sure you want only to open diplomatic contact with us. And—" The Kai paused dramatically; Kira held her breath. "And, perhaps to consult, however briefly, with what you call the Portable-Far-Seeing-Anomaly . . . what we Bajorans call the Orb."

Kira closed her eyes, surprised to feel tears on her cheeks. She leaned back. *The Orb. Of course. What else? Sure, just hand it over; give them our heart, my Kai!*

"We wish no more conflict," said Kai Winn

softly, chillingly. Each word was a pinprick in the back of Kira's tongue, where it joined with the throat. "We offer no more resistance. We will stand and fight no more."

The Kai paused; Kira felt the woman's eyes upon her, and the major opened hers to confront Kai Winn, despair confronting acceptance. "On behalf of the united government of the system of Bajor, I, Kai Winn, hereby surrender this station, *Emissary's Sanctuary*. Unconditionally, and without secret reservation. Treat us kindly, even as you would be treated yourselves, when you come to the Prophets in the fullness of time."

Kai Winn touched a console, and the computer ceased transmitting. "Lower all shields," she said. "Power down all weapons. Transporter room . . . lock onto all of us here in Ops and transport us to the Promenade. We will meet our fate with heads unbowed. Kira?"

Kai Winn reached out and took her reluctant first officer's hand as they dematerialized.

Lieutenant Commmander Worf stood on a small rise, what Captain Sisko had called a "pitcher's mound," evidently a reference to the ancient human game of baseball that obsessed the man. Worf tried not to allow his amazement to show as he surveyed the Terrors of Tiffnaki—the commando squad still commanded by "Mayor-General" Astaha.

For a moment, Worf thought he was looking at a

subbrigade of Klingon warriors that had somehow snuck onto the planet. Their faces were cold and hard, with a faint snarl as they anticipated the coming battle with the Cardassians. They stood in a somewhat ragged line, but they stood proudly . . . both true of typical Klingon warrior groups, who were never known for discipline but rather for ferocity.

"I am proud to serve as your commanding officer," said Worf. He had planned to say it anyway, even if they had turned out to be a ragtag batch of knee-quaking farmers; the Klingon was prepared to swallow his bile and put on "the face." But he was startled to realize that it came out entirely sincere. Worf's own battle lust began to tickle his stomach, and he clenched his fists in anticipation of the first clash, the brittle flicker of battle lines meeting in the red dance.

"We are honored to serve under your command," said Tivva-ma, the young daughter of Asta-ha, who had been selected as the Mouth of Tiff-naki. Every soldier—there were now four hundred, and the mayor-general was away recruiting still more troops—carried a hunk of metal, a wooden club, a sharp stick . . . all the weapons that they had, now that the power grid was off-line across the entire hemisphere. But Worf beamed with pride that they had *taken up the weapons themselves* when their toys abruptly ceased working.

"We thought it was the enemy coming," said Tivva-ma in her charming, brave-little-girl voice.

"When all the stuff stopped working, it was just like when they came before, and the village was attacked, and all those people died, like my daddy. But this time we were gonna use sticks'n'stuff and hurt the bad Cardassians. And we all got the sticks and other stuff. And the Cardassians didn't come, so we came here, and Mom—and Mayor-General Asta-ha started gathering all the other people, and . . . and . . ." She trailed off, as children will when they run out of thoughts.

She saluted, and Worf returned the salute. It was the Klingon salute he had taught them in the initial stages of training, but now the Tiffnakis had earned the privilege of using it. *Though we shall have to adjust Asta-ha's rank downward,* he appended.

"It was not the enemy who turned off all the devices. We did that ourselves—so no more of your fellow defenders will be taken unaware by the Cardassian sabotage."

"We thank you for your, um, new tech of turning off all the tech. But you said there was, um, some other kinds of things we can use to fight the Cardassians. Where are they?"

Where had Jadzia and the *Defiant* gone? *Now would be a good time for her to return,* thought Worf; *they could beam down a few thousand replicated disruptors with internal power supplies.* For the moment, however, Chief O'Brien and the captain were trying to manufacture small cannon out of scrap metal, melting the materials with hand phasers that would not last long at the rate they were using them. "For now, we shall learn the art of fighting with sword and *bat'telh* and the manufacture of bows and the fletching of arrows. We will learn to make spears and javelins." Worf looked over the heads of his audience, seeing not a small subbrigade but a vast army of the future that would defend the planet against any invasion and, ultimately, bring the Natives back to the course of their own natural development. Would Worf of the House of Mogh be hailed as the father of their entire civilization?

Worf foresaw a stockpile of preindustrial weapons for the immediate future, followed by replicated weapons or even manufactured guns, if need be; surely O'Brien could set up a machine shop. After all, in the mists of antiquity, pretechnological Klingon guerrilla warriors from mud hut villages had gunsmithed cheap knockoffs of the machine guns used by their more advanced neighbors during the Wars of First Expansion.

The memory sparked another thought for Commander Worf. "We must begin designing and constructing spring traps and death pits against the invaders. Owena-da will work with O'Brien. You have already learned to forage food in the forests, is that correct?"

"Yes, Commander Worf." Tivva-ma made a strange gesture that Worf thought must be a Sierra-Bravo version of a reverence or curtsy.

"Then you must learn now how to hunt, how to take fish from the rivers, how to grow grain in the fields. You must look not just to winning a battle or two but to winning the war." Remembering a line he had used before, he added, "You must feed the army and also the civilians . . . our battle is to plant crops, and the enemy is time."

Worf began to tremble; whether it was in anticipation of glorious victory or the heady awareness of his own growing political importance, he could not say. But Captain Sisko had silently joined the group and stood now gazing cryptically at the commander from a tree shadow on Worf's right flank. Worf made a mental note: *O'Brien will have to develop a method of extracting the poisons from the planetary food; our own enemy is time as well, time until the* Defiant *returns to orbit and can beam down more supplies.*

"We fight for victory," said Worf, his voice growing naturally quieter. Though a Klingon, he knew his men needed to hear quiet confidence now, not loud boasts. "We fight for honor. We fight—for survival. We cannot go back to the old way of life. There will be *no more tech,* new or old, but what we make ourselves. There will be no attack or defense but what comes from our own sweat and takes from us our own blood.

"But we shall survive . . . and not as children, but as men and women, warriors and growers, builders, not merely finders and players. We will make our lives. We will slaughter our enemies and pile their skulls to the sky for a memorial, but we will build upon that pyramid a world of civilization and progress. And we will touch the stars, my warriors. We will join with the stars."

The silence beat at Worf's ears like a drum. Chief O'Brien, Quark, and Constable Odo had joined Captain Sisko in the shadows. Only Worf stood in the sunlight near the camouflaged Cardassian skimmer, addressing his troops with as much sense of history, he believed, as ever did the first Kahless.

Feeling an unexpected shiver of premonition and hubris, Worf stepped down from the pitcher's mound and joined his comrades under the spreading, blue tree . . .

and process. And we will touch the stars, my
warriors. We will join with the stars."

The [illegible] of Worf's [illegible] Chief
O'Brien, Quark, and Constable Odo had joined
Captain Sisko in the shadows. Only Worf stood in
the spotlight, near the [illegible] Cardassian
[illegible] as [illegible]
in history [illegible] did [illegible] first [illegible]

[illegible]
[illegible]. [illegible] stepped down from the podium's
[illegible] and [illegible] his comrades [illegible] the [illegible]
ing [illegible].

Look for STAR TREK Fiction from Pocket Books

Star Trek®: The Original Series

Star Trek: The Motion Picture • Gene Roddenberry
Star Trek II: The Wrath of Khan • Vonda N. McIntyre
Star Trek III: The Search for Spock • Vonda N. McIntyre
Star Trek IV: The Voyage Home • Vonda N. McIntyre
Star Trek V: The Final Frontier • J. M. Dillard
Star Trek VI: The Undiscovered Country • J. M. Dillard
Star Trek VII: Generations • J. M. Dillard
Star Trek VIII: First Contact • J. M. Dillard
Star Trek IX: Insurrection • J. M. Dillard
Enterprise: The First Adventure • Vonda N. McIntyre
Final Frontier • Diane Carey
Strangers from the Sky • Margaret Wander Bonanno
Spock's World • Diane Duane
The Lost Years • J. M. Dillard
Probe • Margaret Wander Bonanno
Prime Directive • Judith and Garfield Reeves-Stevens
Best Destiny • Diane Carey
Shadows on the Sun • Michael Jan Friedman
Sarek • A. C. Crispin
Federation • Judith and Garfield Reeves-Stevens
The Ashes of Eden • William Shatner & Judith and Garfield Reeves-Stevens
The Return • William Shatner & Judith and Garfield Reeves-Stevens
Star Trek: Starfleet Academy • Diane Carey
Vulcan's Forge • Josepha Sherman and Susan Shwartz
Avenger • William Shatner & Judith and Garfield Reeves-Stevens
Star Trek: Odyssey • William Shatner & Judith and Garfield Reeves-Stevens

#1 *Star Trek: The Motion Picture* • Gene Roddenberry
#2 *The Entropy Effect* • Vonda N. McIntyre
#3 *The Klingon Gambit* • Robert E. Vardeman
#4 *The Covenant of the Crown* • Howard Weinstein
#5 *The Prometheus Design* • Sondra Marshak & Myrna Culbreath
#6 *The Abode of Life* • Lee Correy
#7 *Star Trek II: The Wrath of Khan* • Vonda N. McIntyre

#8 *Black Fire* • Sonni Cooper
#9 *Triangle* • Sondra Marshak & Myrna Culbreath
#10 *Web of the Romulans* • M. S. Murdock
#11 *Yesterday's Son* • A. C. Crispin
#12 *Mutiny on the Enterprise* • Robert E. Vardeman
#13 *The Wounded Sky* • Diane Duane
#14 *The Trellisane Confrontation* • David Dvorkin
#15 *Corona* • Greg Bear
#16 *The Final Reflection* • John M. Ford
#17 *Star Trek III: The Search for Spock* • Vonda N. McIntyre
#18 *My Enemy, My Ally* • Diane Duane
#19 *The Tears of the Singers* • Melinda Snodgrass
#20 *The Vulcan Academy Murders* • Jean Lorrah
#21 *Uhura's Song* • Janet Kagan
#22 *Shadow Lord* • Laurence Yep
#23 *Ishmael* • Barbara Hambly
#24 *Killing Time* • Della Van Hise
#25 *Dwellers in the Crucible* • Margaret Wander Bonanno
#26 *Pawns and Symbols* • Majiliss Larson
#27 *Mindshadow* • J. M. Dillard
#28 *Crisis on Centaurus* • Brad Ferguson
#29 *Dreadnought!* • Diane Carey
#30 *Demons* • J. M. Dillard
#31 *Battlestations!* • Diane Carey
#32 *Chain of Attack* • Gene DeWeese
#33 *Deep Domain* • Howard Weinstein
#34 *Dreams of the Raven* • Carmen Carter
#35 *The Romulan Way* • Diane Duane & Peter Morwood
#36 *How Much for Just the Planet?* • John M. Ford
#37 *Bloodthirst* • J. M. Dillard
#38 *The IDIC Epidemic* • Jean Lorrah
#39 *Time for Yesterday* • A. C. Crispin
#40 *Timetrap* • David Dvorkin
#41 *The Three-Minute Universe* • Barbara Paul
#42 *Memory Prime* • Judith and Garfield Reeves-Stevens
#43 *The Final Nexus* • Gene DeWeese
#44 *Vulcan's Glory* • D. C. Fontana
#45 *Double, Double* • Michael Jan Friedman
#46 *The Cry of the Onlies* • Judy Klass
#47 *The Kobayashi Maru* • Julia Ecklar
#48 *Rules of Engagement* • Peter Morwood
#49 *The Pandora Principle* • Carolyn Clowes

#50 *Doctor's Orders* • Diane Duane
#51 *Enemy Unseen* • V. E. Mitchell
#52 *Home Is the Hunter* • Dana Kramer Rolls
#53 *Ghost-Walker* • Barbara Hambly
#54 *A Flag Full of Stars* • Brad Ferguson
#55 *Renegade* • Gene DeWeese
#56 *Legacy* • Michael Jan Friedman
#57 *The Rift* • Peter David
#58 *Faces of Fire* • Michael Jan Friedman
#59 *The Disinherited* • Peter David
#60 *Ice Trap* • L. A. Graf
#61 *Sanctuary* • John Vornholt
#62 *Death Count* • L. A. Graf
#63 *Shell Game* • Melissa Crandall
#64 *The Starship Trap* • Mel Gilden
#65 *Windows on a Lost World* • V. E. Mitchell
#66 *From the Depths* • Victor Milan
#67 *The Great Starship Race* • Diane Carey
#68 *Firestorm* • L. A. Graf
#69 *The Patrian Transgression* • Simon Hawke
#70 *Traitor Winds* • L. A. Graf
#71 *Crossroad* • Barbara Hambly
#72 *The Better Man* • Howard Weinstein
#73 *Recovery* • J. M. Dillard
#74 *The Fearful Summons* • Denny Martin Flynn
#75 *First Frontier* • Diane Carey & Dr. James I. Kirkland
#76 *The Captain's Daughter* • Peter David
#77 *Twilight's End* • Jerry Oltion
#78 *The Rings of Tautee* • Dean W. Smith & Kristine K. Rusch
#79 *Invasion #1: First Strike* • Diane Carey
#80 *The Joy Machine* • James Gunn
#81 *Mudd in Your Eye* • Jerry Oltion
#82 *Mind Meld* • John Vornholt
#83 *Heart of the Sun* • Pamela Sargent & George Zebrowski
#84 *Assignment: Eternity* • Greg Cox
#85 *Republic:* My Brother's Keeper, Book One • Michael Jan Friedman
#86 *Constitution:* My Brother's Keeper, Book Two • Michael Jan Friedman
#87 *Enterprise:* My Brother's Keeper, Book Three • Michael Jan Friedman

Star Trek: The Next Generation®

Encounter at Farpoint • David Gerrold
Unification • Jeri Taylor
Relics • Michael Jan Friedman
Descent • Diane Carey
All Good Things • Michael Jan Friedman
Star Trek: Klingon • Dean W. Smith & Kristine K. Rusch
Star Trek VII: Generations • J. M. Dillard
Metamorphosis • Jean Lorrah
Vendetta • Peter David
Reunion • Michael Jan Friedman
Imzadi • Peter David
The Devil's Heart • Carmen Carter
Dark Mirror • Diane Duane
Q-Squared • Peter David
Crossover • Michael Jan Friedman
Kahless • Michael Jan Friedman
Star Trek: First Contact • J. M. Dillard
The Best and the Brightest • Susan Wright
Planet X • Michael Jan Friedman

#1 *Ghost Ship* • Diane Carey
#2 *The Peacekeepers* • Gene DeWeese
#3 *The Children of Hamlin* • Carmen Carter
#4 *Survivors* • Jean Lorrah
#5 *Strike Zone* • Peter David
#6 *Power Hungry* • Howard Weinstein
#7 *Masks* • John Vornholt
#8 *The Captains' Honor* • David and Daniel Dvorkin
#9 *A Call to Darkness* • Michael Jan Friedman
#10 *A Rock and a Hard Place* • Peter David
#11 *Gulliver's Fugitives* • Keith Sharee
#12 *Doomsday World* • David, Carter, Friedman & Greenberg
#13 *The Eyes of the Beholders* • A. C. Crispin
#14 *Exiles* • Howard Weinstein
#15 *Fortune's Light* • Michael Jan Friedman
#16 *Contamination* • John Vornholt
#17 *Boogeymen* • Mel Gilden
#18 *Q-in-Law* • Peter David
#19 *Perchance to Dream* • Howard Weinstein

#20 *Spartacus* • T. L. Mancour
#21 *Chains of Command* • W. A. McCay & E. L. Flood
#22 *Imbalance* • V. E. Mitchell
#23 *War Drums* • John Vornholt
#24 *Nightshade* • Laurell K. Hamilton
#25 *Grounded* • David Bischoff
#26 *The Romulan Prize* • Simon Hawke
#27 *Guises of the Mind* • Rebecca Neason
#28 *Here There Be Dragons* • John Peel
#29 *Sins of Commission* • Susan Wright
#30 *Debtors' Planet* • W. R. Thompson
#31 *Foreign Foes* • David Galanter & Greg Brodeur
#32 *Requiem* • Michael Jan Friedman & Kevin Ryan
#33 *Balance of Power* • Dafydd ab Hugh
#34 *Blaze of Glory* • Simon Hawke
#35 *The Romulan Stratagem* • Robert Greenberger
#36 *Into the Nebula* • Gene DeWeese
#37 *The Last Stand* • Brad Ferguson
#38 *Dragon's Honor* • Kij Johnson & Greg Cox
#39 *Rogue Saucer* • John Vornholt
#40 *Possession* • J. M. Dillard & Kathleen O'Malley
#41 *Invasion #2: The Soldiers of Fear* • Dean W. Smith & Kristine K. Rusch
#42 *Infiltrator* • W. R. Thompson
#43 *A Fury Scorned* • Pam Sargent & George Zebrowski
#44 *The Death of Princes* • John Peel
#45 *Intellivore* • Diane Duane
#46 *To Storm Heaven* • Esther Friesner

Q Continuum #1: *Q-Space* • Greg Cox
Q Continuum #2: *Q-Zone* • Greg Cox
Q Continuum #3: *Q-Strike* • Greg Cox

Star Trek: Deep Space Nine®

The Search • Diane Carey
Warped • K. W. Jeter
The Way of the Warrior • Diane Carey
Star Trek: Klingon • Dean W. Smith & Kristine K. Rusch
Trials and Tribble-ations • Diane Carey
Far Beyond the Stars • Steve Barnes
The 34th Rule • Armin Shimerman & David George

#1 *Emissary* • J. M. Dillard
#2 *The Siege* • Peter David
#3 *Bloodletter* • K. W. Jeter
#4 *The Big Game* • Sandy Schofield
#5 *Fallen Heroes* • Dafydd ab Hugh
#6 *Betrayal* • Lois Tilton
#7 *Warchild* • Esther Friesner
#8 *Antimatter* • John Vornholt
#9 *Proud Helios* • Melissa Scott
#10 *Valhalla* • Nathan Archer
#11 *Devil in the Sky* • Greg Cox & John Greggory Betancourt
#12 *The Laertian Gamble* • Robert Sheckley
#13 *Station Rage* • Diane Carey
#14 *The Long Night* • Dean W. Smith & Kristine K. Rusch
#15 *Objective: Bajor* • John Peel
#16 *Invasion #3: Time's Enemy* • L. A. Graf
#17 *The Heart of the Warrior* • John Greggory Betancourt
#18 *Saratoga* • Michael Jan Friedman
#19 *The Tempest* • Susan Wright
#20 *Wrath of the Prophets* • P. David, M. J. Friedman, R. Greenberger
#21 *Trial by Error* • Mark Garland
#22 *Vengeance* • Dafydd ab Hugh

Star Trek®: Voyager™

Flashback • Diane Carey
The Black Shore • Greg Cox
Mosaic • Jeri Taylor

#1 *Caretaker* • L. A. Graf
#2 *The Escape* • Dean W. Smith & Kristine K. Rusch
#3 *Ragnarok* • Nathan Archer
#4 *Violations* • Susan Wright
#5 *Incident at Arbuk* • John Greggory Betancourt
#6 *The Murdered Sun* • Christie Golden
#7 *Ghost of a Chance* • Mark A. Garland & Charles G. McGraw
#8 *Cybersong* • S. N. Lewitt
#9 *Invasion #4: The Final Fury* • Dafydd ab Hugh
#10 *Bless the Beasts* • Karen Haber
#11 *The Garden* • Melissa Scott
#12 *Chrysalis* • David Niall Wilson
#13 *The Black Shore* • Greg Cox
#14 *Marooned* • Christie Golden
#15 *Echoes* • Dean W. Smith & Kristine K. Rusch
#16 *Seven of Nine* • Christie Golden

Star Trek®: New Frontier

#1 *House of Cards* • Peter David
#2 *Into the Void* • Peter David
#3 *The Two-Front War* • Peter David
#4 *End Game* • Peter David
#5 *Martyr* • Peter David
#6 *Fire on High* • Peter David

Star Trek®: Day of Honor

Book One: *Ancient Blood* • Diane Carey
Book Two: *Armageddon Sky* • L. A. Graf
Book Three: *Her Klingon Soul* • Michael Jan Friedman
Book Four: *Treaty's Law* • Dean W. Smith & Kristine K. Rusch

Star Trek®: The Captain's Table

Book One: *War Dragons* • L. A. Graf
Book Two: *Dujonian's Hoard* • Michael Jan Friedman
Book Three: *The Mist* • Dean W. Smith & Kristine K. Rusch
Book Four: *Fire Ship* • Diane Carey
Book Five: *Once Burned* • Peter David
Book Six: *Where Sea Meets Sky* • Jerry Oltion

Star Trek®: The Dominion War

Book 1: *Behind Enemy Lines* • John Vornholt
Book 2: *Call to Arms . . .* • Diane Carey
Book 3: *Tunnel Through the Stars* • John Vornholt
Book 4: *. . . Sacrifice of Angels* • Diane Carey